Listen to Your Spirit

a novel

Kayo Fraser

[signature: Kayo Fraser]

Kayo Fraser
255 N Boulder Rd
Deer Lodge, MT 59722

Raven Publishing
Norris, Montana, USA

Listen to Your Spirit

ISBN: 978-1-937849-53-5
Copyright © 2019 by Kayo Fraser
Cover art and illustrations © 2019 by Janene Grende

Published by Raven Publishing, Inc., P.O. Box 2866, Norris, MT www.ravenpublishing.net

Library of Congress Cataloging-in-Publication Data

Names: Fraser, Kayo, 1948- author.
Title: Listen to your spirit : a novel / Kayo Fraser.
Description: Norris, Montana, USA : Raven Publishing, [2019] | Summary:
 Orphaned after a plane crash in Africa, Florida twelve-year-old Kelly and her ten-year-old brother, Jake, are sold as slaves in South Africa, where Kelly is guided by a mysterious leopard to listen to her spirit.
Identifiers: LCCN 2019005845 | ISBN 9781937849535 (pbk.)
Subjects: | CYAC: Coming of age--Fiction. | Orphans--Fiction. | Brothers and sisters--Fiction. | Slavery--Fiction. | Leopard--Fiction. | South Africa--Fiction.
Classification: LCC PZ7.1.F75453 Lis 2019 | DDC [Fic]--dc23
LC record available at https://lccn.loc.gov/2019005845

Acknowledgments

Many people, including friends, family, writing instructors, fellow writers, and my editors have encouraged me and helped develop my writing skills. Most important are my spirit guides who whisper in my ear when I need help. Thank you all.

A special thanks goes to artist Janene Grende, from Sandpoint, Idaho. Her talent is undeniable, and her friendship is treasured.

Janene has won numerous national competitions and has been well-recognized for her work with Leanin' Tree, Wild Wings, and through her vivid paintings of birds, horses, cowgirls, and wildlife. She is always learning new techniques to improve her work and shares her knowledge with other artists. You can find her paintings in many western galleries and on her web site: *www.janenegrende.com.*

Prologue

When my father first told us he was going to Africa, I was shocked. The thought of my father leaving us made my eyes sting with tears, but when he told my mother we could all go with him, I was terrified—terrified but intrigued. Africa! I imagined a wild country of jungles and lions, of headhunters with spears. True, I didn't know much about that continent, but it was never a place I thought I'd visit.

The potpourri of emotions I was feeling was hard to sort through. Part of me looked forward to seeing something new and different. I guess that was the adventurous part of me, but my insecurities as a twelve-year-old girl filled me with doubts and fears I couldn't imagine living in a hut in the jungle. What about my friends? I'd be leaving them all behind. What would I do? Who would I play with, beside my pesky little brother?

Our family lived in Florida, near Orlando. My father, Gene Conner, was a doctor of internal medicine. He became interested in pediatrics after I was born and went back to college to get another degree.

He was fascinated with the infections caused by

bacteria, viruses, fungi, and parasites. If I had an ear infection, Dad wanted to know what it was and where it came from. We always had to put alcohol in our ears after swimming in the local ponds and swimming pools. He was responsible for closing a lake to swimming one time when he discovered a parasite in the water. If this parasite entered the body through the nasal passage, it could travel to the brain, which was often fatal. Florida gave Dad a lot of microscopic life forms to study.

The same thing was true for my mother. She was a botanist and found a myriad of plants and other organisms to study in the state. She and my father met in college. She preferred studying natural medicine, whereas Dad took more of the scientific approach.

One evening after dinner Dad said, 'Lizzie, what do you think about me going to Uganda for a year and a half?' Mom's name was Elizabeth, but Dad called her Lizzie or sometimes Liz. He asked the question in a matter-of-fact tone as if he wanted to know what she thought about the weather.

Mom stopped reading the paper and looked over at him to see if he was joking.

He explained, "There is a non-profit group called *For the Kids* that sends doctors, nurses, and other volunteers to impoverished countries that desperately need medical assistance. Uganda is one of many and on the top of this list right now.

I can still picture him sitting there in the living room. His dark brown hair had a few highlights of gray around his temples, which intensified his penetrating gray-blue eyes. If he looked at you disapprovingly, you wanted to crawl in a hole to avoid his glare. He was kind, but down to earth in his approach to everything in life. He laughed but not often. Dad took life more seriously than Mom, which made them a good contrast to each other.

I remember the look on my mother's face. When she got excited, it looked like sparks of light welled up deep inside her to shine through her hazel-green eyes like a twin set of light beams. Her eyes gleamed when she said, "That'd be great, but only if you take us with you."

Dad said, "I was hoping you would say that, but I didn't expect you to be so enthused."

"Are you kidding?" she said. "I'd have the chance to see what grows in another country; to study other healing herbs. I think it'd be a great experience for the kids too," she said, looking at my brother and me. "When will you know for sure?"

Dad told us there'd be thousands of sick and dying children, many of them orphaned when their parents fell ill and died of AIDS, hepatitis, cholera, dysentery, malaria, and other infectious diseases.

We'd all need to be vaccinated before leaving, and when we got there, we would live in a hut just like the rest of the villagers.

My brother, Jake, thought this would be a great way to get out of school and was all for it. I was reluctant, but couldn't help but get excited the more we talked about it.

Mom said we'd have to keep up with our studies so she would home-school us. I believe she was also thinking about sharing some schoolwork with the kids in the villages.

Dad pointed out this wouldn't be a vacation, and he expected us to help in the clinic after our lessons.

We talked about it a little more, and all agreed to go in spite of his warnings about the horrors of the diseases and the limited facilities in the villages. I was almost twelve years old. Jake was ten. It started out to be an adventurous family trip.

We flew to Entebbe, Uganda. A guide met us at the luggage carousel and took us to a hotel for the night.

I was tired from the long trip but excited about the sights and smells of this strange country. I don't think my head hit the pillow before I was asleep.

The next morning we boarded a small, chartered airplane that was hired to take us to the village where my father would work for the next eighteen months.

The pilot said the monsoons had started early that year and it would be a rough flight. I wasn't sure where the little village was since it was too small to show on any of the maps.

Once we were in the air, I watched the sprawling city change to patchwork farms, then the terrain changed to the Savannah grasslands, then to dark clusters of trees. I was being lulled to sleep by the rain on the windows and the steady vibration of the engines—until they stopped! The quiet stillness was ominous.

I knew something was wrong—terribly wrong.

Chapter 1

I was afraid to open my eyes as I tried to sort through my confusion. Surreal images and screams flooded my mind, creating a nightmare so terrifying I feared it might be real. The acrid smell of smoke burned my nostrils, and my head throbbed as if it'd been split open. I wanted to believe I was still safe in my bedroom in Florida, but I was not convinced. I wanted to go back to sleep and change the dream to one less painful. I hoped to hear my mother gently call, "Wake up Kelly."

Instead of my soft, cozy bed, I felt the hard, damp ground beneath me. I shivered with the cold realization that I was not safe at home.

"Wake up Kelly." It was not my mother's sweet voice calling to me.

"Kelly?" the distant voice whispered. "Kelly?" the voice said a bit louder. "Wake up! Are you okay? You have to wake up! I'm scared!" The urgent sound of Jake's voice penetrated my foggy mind.

"Wha-a-t?" My voice was weak and shaky. "What happened?"

As I slowly opened my eyes the fog in my mind lifted a little. The first thing I saw looming over me was a broken wing of the airplane. Rain dripped off the wing, creating puddles of water all around me. Smoke lifted beyond the thick curtain of trees, only a little patch of gray sky peeked through the dark, damp branches. The crackling of a small, distant fire and the smell of burnt wire penetrated my consciousness. I coughed and sat upright. The sudden movement left me dizzy. I lifted my hands to my head and felt a lump the size of a walnut. I was relieved to see there was no blood on my hands.

"Jake? Jake, where are you?"

"Kelly! You're awake! Thank God. I was afraid... you were..." His voice trailed off as his shoulders shook with his silent sobs.

"What happened?" I asked again.

"We were in a plane crash, remember?"

The loud patter of heavy rain hissed as it fell on the still burning fuselage of what had been a single engine Cessna. The surrounding jungle was too wet to catch fire from the burning plane. Flames crackled then sputtered as the downpour drowned the blaze.

"Where're Mom and Dad?"

"I don't know," Jake answered. "You're the first person I've seen."

In a flash, I remembered hearing the pilot's

steady voice as he spoke into the microphone, giving some sort of bearings for their flight plan. Then I heard him shout, "Mayday, Mayday! This is Charlie two zero six...plane going down north northwest..." The pilot never finished his call. Then the airplane jerked, and I was tossed forward. The world spun around, and there was a loud explosion.

I rubbed my eyes trying to clear my mind.

"We have to find Mom and Dad," I cried.

I wanted to hear my mother's soothing voice saying everything was okay. There had been a loud scream before everything faded into quiet darkness. I didn't know if the scream was mine or the last sound I would ever hear from my mother.

My senses were starting to clear. Jake was on his hands and knees trying to get up. His once sandy-colored hair was wet and soaked with blood. He had several scratches on his face that looked like they were connecting the dots of his freckles. He looked at me with wide, red-rimmed eyes. Tears stained his flushed, sooty cheeks. The look of terror in his eyes made me bolt to my feet and run to him. I tripped over cushions and suitcases that had been thrown from the plane.

"Are you okay?" I demanded.

I had never seen him look so frightened and beaten. He was tough for a ten-year-old, but my instinct to care for my younger brother overshadowed the thoughts of my own condition. I couldn't think beyond the look on his face—the dark pits of fear in his hazel-green eyes. I tore my gaze from him to the wreckage littered around us.

The bottom and left side of the airplane had split open exposing what little remained inside the passenger compartment. I vaguely remembered being tossed through the opening like a rag doll. The right wing was still attached to the plane, but the tail section had snapped off. There were broken branches strewn around the plane from the treetops that had been mowed down as the aircraft dropped out of the sky. A furrow of plowed dirt where the plane skidded to a stop on the soft, wet, mossy ground released an earthy fragrance, overpowered by the smell of burnt rubber and electric wiring. A sickening smell of singed hair filled my nose as we stared in disbelief at the place where our parents had been sitting in the plane.

"Mom? Dad? Where are you?" I screamed. "Jake? Do you see them?" Fear was so tight in my throat, I could hardly speak as the realization sank in that we had crashed in the jungle and might be the only survivors. Tears formed in my eyes and burned my cheeks as they streamed down my face.

"Oh, God! No! Not Mom and Dad?" The look in

my brother's eyes matched my own feeling of terror. Jake barely managed to stand and half walked, half crawled to the wreckage. "Do you think they're still inside?"

The fumes from the burning wires seared my throat, and I could hardly speak. I was afraid to step any closer to the plane for fear of what I'd see inside. I spoke more to myself than to Jake, hoping to clear my mind and settle the nausea that swelled inside me. "Dad sat in the seat to the right of the pilot and Mom sat in the first seat behind him. You and I were on the left side of the plane. The pilot must've hit some trees that opened up our side of the plane and threw us out. It looks like the plane landed on the nose and fell to the right side. Look around just in case they were thrown out of the plane like we were." I stepped slowly into the bowels of the airplane, blinking back tears from the smoldering fire in the cockpit.

The pilot lay slumped over the control panel. The windshield had showered him with tiny shards of glass and a wound in his neck was caked with blood so dark it was almost black. The seat where my father was sitting folded around him and crushed him between the seat and the dash.

The horror of seeing my father and the pilot was overwhelming. I couldn't hold back the vomit. I emptied my stomach and continued to vomit until there was nothing left but dry heaves.

Then I realized I had not yet found my mother. "Please, God, don't take my mother, too. Please let her be okay."

Tears filled my eyes once again as I remembered something my mother once told me, 'God answers all our prayers, but sometimes the answer is 'No.'"

And that day God said "No" to my prayers. Mom's body had been tossed to the rear of the plane. Her arms and legs were twisted in impossible positions. I could only stare, frozen—not really seeing at all. The light that had once shone in her eyes was gone. Never had I seen a dead person before, but now there was no doubt about what death looked like.

I closed my eyes tight to shut out the sight of my dead and mangled parents. Grief overwhelmed me as I fell in a heap sobbing so violently that I dry heaved again. I could hardly breathe as the contractions in my stomach tightened around my lungs. My throat was sore, but I swallowed the bile and took a breath of air.

Gasping, I sat up and looked around for my brother. He hadn't moved when I told him to search for survivors. He just stood there staring at me.

"You don't have to say it. I know. I know. Don't say it, please." I stepped out of the plane as he ran to me. We wrapped our arms around each other and cried. "I wish I'd died, too," he said.

Never had we experienced death. Never had we been left alone. But here we were deep in the jungle, no sight or sound from any villages, towns, or other people to help us.

Through all the tears and fears, at some point, the survival instinct kicked in. I had to stop crying for now and assess the situation. As I pulled away, Jake shuddered then asked, "D-do, do you think anyone can find us? How long before someone will know we are missing?"

"I don't know, Jake. I heard the pilot talking on the radio just before we crashed. I think we should stay here just in case someone saw the plane go down. Go see if you can find any dry wood. It will be dark soon, and we'll need a fire. The smoke might help someone find us," I added.

Oh, yeah," he said, still sounding dazed. "Remember when Dad took us camping? I loved watching the firelight flicker on the leaves around us. It made me feel safe and warm." A tear formed in his eyes and he wiped it away with the back of his hand. "A fire will be nice to keep the wild animals away, too."

"Wild animals? I hadn't thought of that," I said staring into the dense jungle.

While Jake gathered firewood, I searched the rubble for something we could use. The belly of the plane had been torn open by the treetops just before it crashed. All the cargo fell out, and some of the boxes split open when they hit the trees, dumping their contents on the jungle floor. Stenciled on the sides of several boxes were the words 'Dr. Eugene Connor, Uganda'. I ran my fingers over my father's name.

In the boxes were medical supplies he planned to use at the village. I didn't know anything about the medicines, but I did find a survival kit that would be helpful. *What luck!* I almost laughed at the irony of my thought. I sighed realizing luck was desperately needed at this time more than we had ever needed it before.

My father always took a survival kit of some sort whenever he went to the backcountry. "You need to be prepared for the unexpected," he told me.

"I don't think he would have ever expected a plane crash like this!" I half laughed and half cried, sorting through the large red and white plastic box.

Among the emergency items were a fire-starting flint and tinder, a compass, tablets to purify drinking water, four canteens and four small compressed packages of aluminum thermal blankets.

We'll sure need these for our beds in this sopping wet jungle. I thought.

The first camping trip with our parents, I had rolled my eyes wondering why anyone would want to go out into the wilderness and sleep on the cold, hard ground, but to my surprise, I loved it and enjoyed looking for the treasures that Mother Nature provided. My mother showed me how to find wild strawberries and raspberries. I could build a fire, pitch a tent and identify useful plants for teas. Back then, I never dreamed that my life would depend on that knowledge.

Chapter 2

The night was filled with grief, worry, and noises that I couldn't identify. The fire Jake built added the comfort of light, which kept the animals away as we tried to sleep. The strange noises that crept and crawled at the edge of the firelight during the night changed with the morning light. The birds squawked at us from above. I didn't know if they chattered at us or at other visitors we couldn't see.

I opened my eyes to the new morning and looked around, trying to assess our situation. Jake was still asleep. With his eyes closed, he looked so peaceful. I hated to wake him but thought we should make some decisions about what to do. The rain had stopped during the night, but no sun shone through the dense forest growth.

"Jake? Jake are you awake?"

"I am now," he replied as he slowly focused on my face. "Oh, shoot. I was hoping I was just having a bad dream, but it really did happen, didn't it? We were in a plane crash, huh?"

"Yeah. It looks like the plane just fell out of the

sky. Something must have gone wrong with the engine, and the plane sort of glided toward the ground until it got hung up in the trees and fell. If we had flown full-power straight into the mountain, we probably wouldn't be alive."

"So you think that's a good thing?" Jake said, "Being alive out here in who knows where? Alone?"

"We're not alone. We have each other, and there must be some reason we're alive. Mom always said, 'Look for the good in everything, and that's what you'll find.'"

"Well, I don't see too many good things right now."

I wanted to ignore his remark, but I had to agree. Our situation was perilous with little hope it would get better, but my instincts were to find something positive to say. "Well, we have lots of supplies and could stay alive for weeks if we had to. Maybe that'll give someone time to find us."

"I don't want to spend another night here," Jake said. "I don't think anyone knows where we are, and I can't stand to stay any longer so close to..." He couldn't finish the sentence, but I understood what he was thinking. I didn't like to be so close to the dead bodies of our parents, either. It was painful and a little creepy.

Jake looked toward the cockpit, and his eyes reddened as he fought the tears that threatened to flow. I wrapped my arms around him, and we cried once again. It was a toss-up which emotion was worse, the grief of losing our parents or the fear of what would happen to us next.

"Let's see what we can use and put it in a pile," I suggested. "We can sort through it all and choose what to take with us if we have to hike out of here."

I found my suitcase and changed into clean, dry clothes and grabbed a couple pair of shorts, short sleeved shirts, a long-sleeved shirt, several pairs of socks and underwear. Next, I found my mother's suitcase—and hesitated about opening it. It was surreal to be going through her bags, but it was necessary in case there was anything to help with our survival. There were several boxes of protein bars and packages of nuts, hard candy and beef jerky that I took out. Tucked under my mother's neatly folded clothes was a small package wrapped in a brightly colored cloth with a matching purple silk ribbon—a birthday present! The card read, "To my darling daughter. Love, Mom."

My parents promised a party for my twelfth birthday after we got to the village. I could imagine the smile on my mother's face as she wrapped the gift. I didn't want to let go of that image. The realization that this was the last present I would ever receive from my mother made me sob so violently my whole body shook. Whatever was inside this box was not as valuable as the thought that created it. I stuck the present in my pocket and thought, *maybe later, but I don't want to open it now.*

My survival instincts shoved grief into the deeper folds of my mind as I grabbed Mom's purse. It was more of a backpack than a purse. Mom said, "It helps to keep my hands free for other things, and I can carry more stuff in it when we travel."

With a heaviness in my chest, I dumped the contents onto a shirt placed on the ground. It was hard to believe that we were laughing together yesterday.

All four passports were in a water-proof bag. These documents would be the only connection we would have to the world we left behind in the States, and hopefully, they would help us get home. There were some cheese crackers with peanut butter in them, packages of tissues, a couple bottles of water which we would need. The other personal items, I decided not to take. Mom didn't wear much makeup. She didn't need to. She was naturally beautiful with a perpetual tan and hazel-green eyes surrounded in dark lashes and eyebrows.

I put the snacks, passports, Mom's precious gift, and a change of clothes in the backpack.

By mid-morning, we had a large pile of supplies.

"This is way too much stuff," I said. "Let's pick out only what we can carry for food, water, and making a campfire for cooking and boiling water if we need to. I'll take the survival kit in my bag. We'll have to get along without a change of clothes. You take the compass; you're good at reading it," I told Jake. "Which direction do you think we should go?"

"Well, I think we should go downhill," Jake replied. "That direction is ah...east. It'll be easier to walk that way. Maybe we can find some animal trails. I just hope we don't run into any dangerous animals!" Jake said.

I had to laugh. Not because what Jake said was funny, but laughter seemed to ease my fears. "Dad always said, 'The only thing to fear is fear itself.'"

"I'm not afraid," Jake said. I knew he was trying to be brave. Then he continued. "But I wonder if Dad meant not to fear lions, tigers, gorillas, snakes, and who knows what else is out there?"

"You can stop worrying about tigers. There aren't any in Africa unless you go to a zoo or something."

"Well, thank goodness for small favors," he said sarcastically.

With choices made about what we could carry and a last look at the wreckage, we started our trek off the mountain hoping to find a village for help.

Travel was slow. It was difficult to choose a path

with all the entwining animal trails. We tried one trail but had to double back to find a better route through the thick, broad leaves of the jungle. So much water dripped from the trees, it sounded like it was still raining, leaving the ground wet and slippery.

The pungent smell of rotting earth mingled with a sweet herbal fragrance from the plants we crushed beneath our feet was refreshing. But the misery from the monsoon was heightened when the stinging bugs came out in full force. They escaped most of our swats, and their numbers were too great even if we had killed the ones buzzing around our necks and faces. The birds and small animals in the trees fluttered and squawked overhead. The forest was so thick it was impossible to see whether they were squirrels, monkeys, or something else in the tree-tops. The birds were easy to identify if only by their sounds. Their melodic tunes were almost soothing. Had our circumstances been different, I would have enjoyed listening to them. "Like music to my ears," Mom often said.

We walked for hours in the dark green wilderness, and night approached swiftly. The monumental task before us was starting to sink in. I wanted to pray for someone to find us, but I didn't want to give God any more reason to say "No" to me. I was too tired to cry. I told Jake, "Let's make camp here in the clearing. There's room to lay down the space tarps, and we can build a fire."

"I'm glad we brought some of those twigs from last night," Jake said. "There's nothing here dry enough to start a fire. Everything's wet, including me."

The fire felt good, not only for the drying warmth, but the crackling flames danced off the jungle branches creating a cave of light that seemed to protect us from the animals that hunt at night.

"I don't know if I am more hungry or more tired!" Jake said. He had done most of the work blazing the trail and choosing the path. He was two years younger than me but a couple inches taller. He loved hiking and had a natural instinct for direction, but the trails didn't always go east, making it hard to follow the compass, "I hope I'm right about which way to travel."

We made a broth in our metal cups over the fire with some jerky in water. Too tired to worry about the night sounds, we fell fast asleep.

Morning came before I was rested. All the bumps and tumbles from the airplane's sudden landing and my hitting the ground revisited my body now that the shock of the accident had worn off. The stress of our situation had masked the pain until this morning. I groaned as I rolled over to get up. Jake woke up so fast he flung his arms out and almost hit me.

"What? What's the matter?" he asked.

"I'm okay, just a bit stiff and sore." I lied about the extent of my injuries, thinking they might be worse than I wanted to admit. I dreaded facing another day in the jungle alone. I had Jake, and that was a great comfort, but I still felt alone.

Jake added a little wood to the fire, but everything was too wet to do anything more than smoke. "Here, have some dried apples," Jake offered. We ate breakfast in silence then drank some of the precious water still in the canteens.

"Okay, we won't get anywhere sitting here," I said. "Let's head out. I'll clear the trail today." I hoped more activity would take the soreness out of my body, or maybe the exhaustion from work would help me sleep at night.

Another day passed, and another. I lost count of how many days we traveled. Our progress was slow, and many times we had to double back when the trail came to a dead end. We were both tired, and I was weak, so we only walked a few hours each day.

Our food rations were running low, and the water was almost gone. We filled the canteens when we could from the clear mountain streams and where water gathered in the large jungle leaves. No rain had fallen in a couple days, so there wasn't much to collect.

"We need to find some fresh water," Jake said. His words were slurred and sounded thick as he spoke. Dark circles formed under his eyes and his eyelids drooped heavily. His hair was dirty, and his clothes were torn. I figured I probably looked as bad.

A few strips of dried meat was all we had left to eat. The little fruit we found was hardly enough to fill our stomachs.

"We need to rest," I sighed. "I can't take another step without more sleep. Let's make camp and stay an extra day to rest up."

I secretly prayed for someone to help us, anyone, as I gratefully fell into a sleep so deep it was hard to tell the difference between life and the death that seemed so close; a place where only dreams are found.

There before me was a large black leopard. A leopard? I was too tired to be frightened. The leopard didn't seem dangerous. He just stood there, slowly fanning his tail as if waiting for something. What could a leopard want with me? *I thought.*

My mother had told me, "If you want to know something, ask. Nobody can read your mind."

So I asked, "What can I do for you?"

The leopard stepped closer.

"What do you want?" I asked a little louder think-

ing it was hard of hearing.

The leopard just stood there looking at me.

Feeling a little annoyed that my questions were being ignored, I thought, How rude! When someone speaks to you, you should answer.

What are you doing here? I asked.

"That is the first question you have asked that I can answer." The leopard finally replied in a deep growl.

The voice came from the animal but more as a thought than as words from his mouth. I had not expected the leopard to speak. When he did, I was surprised.

"Well? What are you doing here?" I repeated.

"You asked for me to come," the leopard replied.

"I did? How could I? I don't know you!"

"You know me," the leopard growled softly. "You asked for someone to help you, so I came. I have always been close by, but you have not asked for me until now."

"Well? Can you get us out of here? Can you take us home?" I asked hopefully.

"I am here to help, but you must find your own way home," the leopard said.

I didn't see how this leopard could help me. He stood there promising to help, but then he said I had to help myself. I don't get it, I thought.

"*Well, then help me!*" *I cried.*

"*What help do you want?*" *the leopard asked.*

"*What do you mean, what help do I want? Isn't it obvious?*"

"*You must ask for what you want,*" *the leopard patiently stated.* "*I cannot guess.*"

"*What help do I want? I want someone to find us and take us away from here,*" *I said in disbelief that the leopard could not figure out something so obvious.*

"Kelly! Kelly!" Jake shouted. "Kelly! Someone's coming!"

"Help!" He hollered, "Over here! Over here! We're saved Kelly; we're saved!"

Jake was so excited he couldn't stand still. He ran towards the sound of men slicing through the underbrush.

I sat up rubbing my eyes. I wasn't sure which dream was real, the leopard or the people crashing through the brush. I could hear voices in the distance and slashing of metal against wood as if an army was cutting through the jungle coming to rescue us.

Rescue? Rescue? Someone was coming to rescue us! Someone must have found the plane and followed our trail. *Oh, thank goodness.*

I could barely sit up and discovered I was in

a worse condition than I realized. I had given my brother a larger proportion of the food and water, figuring there might not be enough for both of us to survive, and if Jake could keep his strength he would be able to get out of here even if I couldn't.

I didn't have the strength to shout. But Jake was making enough noise for both of us.

Finally, it's over, and we can go home.

In my exhaustion, I had forgotten there was no home to go to. Any home we'd had in the past crashed with the plane. We weren't out of the jungle yet, but at least we were rescued.

God finally answered my prayer. I don't know if I spoke those words aloud or just thought them.

A nagging thought ran through my mind—something my mother often said, "Be careful what you wish for, it might come true."

Why did I have to think of that? I asked myself. *What could possibly be wrong with being rescued?*

Chapter 3

The first live humans we had seen in a long time, came rushing through the jungle. There were two dark-skinned natives and two white men behind them. Jake ran towards the rescue party. I sat and waited for them to come to me.

When the men approached, I thought it was odd that the native men wore the same clothes that my father had. Then I fainted.

When I next opened my eyes, staring at me were the most intense eyes I'd ever seen. It was like looking into the darkness of night with gold flecks of light at the edges of this man's pupils.

I could hear Jake telling the men what had happened, and asking them how they'd found us. He didn't seem to notice I'd been unconscious until the tall man said, "Girl sick. Fever. I get medicine." He set his pack down and disappeared into the jungle for what seemed a long time. The other guide started a fire and placed a pot over the flames.

Jake came over to me with a worried look on his face. "Are you okay Sis?"

"I'll be all right," I tried to reassure him.

"It's a miracle you two survived that crash," the tall, thin white man said. "My name is Marcel Solange. My partner here is Gustave Reynaud—he goes by Gus—and the other two chaps are Simba—the one who went into the jungle looking for his type of medicine—and this here is Kibwe. They are from Uganda. We hired them as our guides because they know how to get around in this jungle like it's their backyard. Come to think of it—it is their backyard!" He laughed.

"We figured it was a couple of kids by the clothes we found, but we didn't expect to find you alive," he continued. "There are lots of things out there that would just as soon eat you as to look at you." He chuckled. "You two are very lucky."

I couldn't tell where the two white men were from by their accents, but that was okay; we were rescued. That's all that mattered.

Simba reappeared carrying a handful of what looked like weeds and leaves. He placed them into the pot of water Kibwe had set by the fire to boil. "Good for fever," he explained. "Two days, then travel."

"Two days?" Jake said. "Well, what're two days, when we've been lost for what seems like weeks? Do you have anything to eat?"

The white men started a fire while the natives disappeared into the jungle. They returned with some animal, skinned and ready to cook for dinner, and a hand full of what appeared to be roots. The one pot with the herbs was brewing near the fire, and another pot was placed over the fire with the fresh meat and roots.

"Whatever that animal was doesn't matter," Jake said. "I'm so hungry, I could eat a monkey raw."

Gus gave a sideways glance at Marcel and laughed. He said something I didn't understand, which made me uncomfortable.

Simba poured some of the hot liquid into a cup and came over to where I was resting.

"Drink," he said as I scooted up to lean against a tree. "Make you strong."

His skin was dark, like black velvet, and his eyes, like those of a wild animal, held my attention. I couldn't help but stare. There was something familiar about those eyes, almost hypnotic. I was a little frightened but too weak to do anything other than accept his offering of tea.

I sipped the hot, bitter drink then coughed. Simba waited until I drank it all before he left. I soon fell asleep. What may have been a few hours later, I woke up feeling much better and sat up. Everyone else must have eaten and were busy making camp. Jake brought some of the stew to me. I was famished and ate everything in the bowl not caring what it was, then I rolled over on my side. Before falling asleep again, I heard Jake ask, "Will she be okay?" The only reply he got was a grunt.

"What was in that tea?" he asked Simba. But he didn't even get a grunt that time.

Simba made me a bed of soft twigs and branches then placed my aluminum blanket over those. He stretched a rope from the tree to make a lean-to with a tarp that had probably been his own shelter. Jake crawled in next to me.

It was barely light when I woke up in the morning. Jake was still asleep. It had started to rain again sometimes during the night. The water poured off the broad leaves and formed little rivulets that ran into my meager shelter. I was cold and wet.

Simba saw I was awake and brought me a cup of hot broth left over from the previous night's meal. The warmth was a welcome treat. He wanted to stay another day, but it was apparently not his decision to make. The white men seemed to be arguing around the breakfast fire.

Simba and Kibwe fashioned a large sling with a set of handles on the front and a second set on the back. Simba picked me up and gently placed me on the carrier. He and Kibwe carried me, while the other two men led the way. I felt better but was still weak and grateful that I didn't have to walk. I was happy this nightmare was soon to be over.

Jake was the last one on the trail, walking behind me. There was still a lot of underbrush, so he had to struggle to keep up. The path took us uphill in the general direction we had come but more direct, unlike the switchback routes Jake and I had taken. It was discouraging to go back to where we started after we had worked hard for several days to get out of there.

Surprisingly it only took one full day for us to return to the crash. I felt nauseated just remembering what had happened here a few days ago. My heart beat heavily, and my eyes filled with tears. I dreaded seeing the plane again, knowing the horror of my dead parents inside.

When the men put down my carrier, I crawled off, stood up, and walked toward the crash site. I still felt dizzy and weak, but I had to look around one last time. Everything was different. All the suitcases and boxes of medical supplies were gone. The plane had been stripped of everything usable; even the wings had been removed. I stared at what was left of the wreckage hardly recognizing it had ever been an airplane. Then I realized the three bodies were gone.

"We buried," Simba explained in broken English.

"Yeah, we didn't want the lions to get used to human flesh," Gus laughed. "Besides it was stinking too bad to strip the plane."

I looked around for the graves. Gus pointed to the far side of the little clearing. There were three mounds with three slabs stuck in the ground serving as headstones.

"Which one is…" Jake started to ask.

"Woman in middle," Simba nodded. "Men are buried as in plane. No know who wife was so she in middle."

We then knew our father was buried to our right.

"I want to make grave markers," Jake said as he reached into his pants pocket for his jackknife. He pulled up the wood slab to the right and carved *Dad* and placed it back in the ground. He carved *Mom* for the middle grave, and since we didn't know the pilot's name, he carved *Pilot* for his grave to the left.

We didn't know much about praying over the dead, but we said our goodbyes and cried. I missed our parents so very much and still couldn't believe they were gone, but I was relieved that their bodies had been buried.

My whole life, up to now, was buried in the dirt in front of me. I cried and hugged my brother. *What will become of us?*

I looked around for flowers to put on the graves

and saw some up in the trees. I tried to pick them, but they were too high to reach. Jake saw me look up and knew what was in my mind, but Simba came over, and told us, "Bad. Pretty, but bad," was all he said. So we didn't pick the flowers. His warning was clear.

Simba reached into a pocket of his pants and sprinkled what looked like tobacco on the three graves. He said something in his native language and walked away. The shirt he wore was the one my father had worn for special occasions.

"That's the shirt Dad was going to wear for my party!" I whispered to Jake.

At first, I was angry that he stole my father's shirt, but then I figured my dad wouldn't need it now. I was glad that if anyone had it, Simba did. I was grateful to him for giving me the tea. The shirt was a small payment for saving my life.

Jake searched around and found our suitcases tossed upside down in the brush. The clothes were damp but not soaking wet. The clothes I'd been wearing were badly torn and stiff with caked mud. Jake had already put on a fresh shirt and pants, but I waited until the dark of night to change my clothes.

I slept better that night than I had in a long time. Even the mysterious jungle sounds didn't keep me awake. We were safe now, and I could relax a little.

Chapter 4

Before daylight peeked through the trees, the men were busy tearing down camp and redistributing the supplies that were left.

"The porters took most of the salvageable parts from the airplane, already," Marcel explained. "We need the sling you were in, to carry out the rest of the supplies. Can you walk, girl?"

"I'm fine," I replied. *More power to them*, I thought. I didn't care about anything but getting back to civilization. I felt stronger today than I had since the crash. For the first time since this nightmare began, I had hope. Jake and I both grabbed a few more clothes and a pair of sandals and placed them in our backpacks. There wasn't much else to take.

Simba had made another stew for our breakfast, and as soon as we were through eating, the men were ready to go.

There were still many questions to ask: *Where are they taking us? What will we do when we get there—where ever* there *was?*

I didn't want to engage in any conversations with the white men. They might have rescued us, but they made me feel uncomfortable the way they looked at me with crooked smiles. Simba didn't look directly at me, and he didn't speak English very well, so I didn't think he would be able to tell me much. The other native only spoke words I didn't understand.

We walked southwest, according to Jake's compass. So we had been wrong about the direction we thought would be the way out of here, but that was behind us now. I wondered how long it would take to get to civilization.

When we stopped for a quick lunch, Gus explained, "We heard the airplane overhead. Then there was an explosion and a puff of smoke, probably when it struck the trees. We figured we should see if there were any survivors even though we didn't expect there to be any. Who lives through a plane crash?" He laughed, raising his arms in a shrug.

The path we took away from the wreckage was apparently the same one the porters used to haul out the salvaged airplane parts. The trail was wide, well-worn, and easy to travel. I could smell the fresh dirt and pungent aroma from the broken branches and bruised plants they trampled. Simba found some fruit just off the trail that he shared with Jake and me. I took special note of what was edible, just in case I ever needed that information in the future. *You never know,* I said to myself.

By late afternoon the foliage had changed. The trees weren't as tall nor as plentiful, and there were grassy patches now. A few rays of sun filtered through the gray clouds and touched my face. It had been weeks since I'd last seen sunlight. Most of our travels had been in an airplane or in the rain. It had been cloudy in Florida a few days before we left, so the warmth of the sun felt wonderful, even in the damp heat.

I remembered packing for this trip with my mother, trying to decide what to take.

"You won't need much for clothing," Mom said. "Take shorts, a couple pairs of long pants, a few tops, a long sleeve shirt, and a light jacket. The climate will be much like it is here in Florida, but it will rain much more during the monsoon season. Take a few pairs of socks and two pair of sandals. You can wear your sneakers while we travel. We will buy what you and your brother need when we get to Entebbe. You might want to take a deck of cards for the trip. Leave your photos here; they will just get destroyed in the rain. We will be gone for about eighteen months, so take only the things you think you will need: toothbrush, hair brush, comb, and maybe some of those pretty hair clips. The village people will enjoy seeing butterflies in your hair," she laughed.

The sound of my mother's laughter was like mu-

sic to my ears and my heart soared now, just remembering. Mom was almost five feet four inches tall, petite, but energetic. Her thick blond hair flowed over her shoulders like a cape when it was not tied back in a ribbon or hair clip. Her hazel eyes looked through thick dark lashes and seemed always to shine like she had a funny joke to tell.

"I'm so excited about going to a foreign country, Mom! I can hardly believe it!" I said eagerly.

"Me too!" Mom laughed. "It's not just a foreign country but a different continent with many countries in it. Like North America has the United States, Canada, and Mexico, to name a few—one continent with a few countries. Africa has fifty-four countries on one continent. We'll learn about that after we get there. I love adventures, don't you? It keeps life interesting."

Chapter 5

"Kelly," Jake whispered. "Kelly, are you awake? Shhhhh."

"Yes, Jake," I whispered back, "what it is?"

"I'm happy we got rescued," Jake confided, "but I don't trust these men. They keep talking in that foreign language and looking at us." Jake didn't seem to realize that their language was not foreign; we were the foreigners.

"If they take us to a town or village we can ask someone for help," I assured him. "I don't know how, but we'll get back to the States, I promise. Maybe we can find a phone and call Aunt Emma. She'll know what to do."

I wondered if anyone had missed us yet. Mom had called home before we got on the small airplane in Entebbe knowing there would not be phone service where we were going. It would probably be weeks or months before anyone knew we were missing.

During breakfast, I asked Marcel, "Where are you taking us, sir? Will we be able to call home? I'm sure my aunt and uncle are worried about us." I lied a little, hoping the men would figure someone would be looking for us. "They'll probably give you a big reward for finding us," I added, hoping the reward would inspire the men to find a telephone on our behalf.

"Don't worry your pretty little head," Marcel replied. "We're meeting a ship on the Kagera River and will put you and your brother on board."

I was relieved to hear Marcel say he would give us free passage home. *What a nice man*, I thought. *How lucky to be rescued by someone who will help us.*

"Jake, did you hear that? We'll be going home, soon."

"Yeah, I heard what he said. I can't wait to get out of this jungle. I hope I never have to see any part of Africa again."

The next few days of travel were much easier. The rain stopped, and the sun burned rays through the clouds in streaks. I was tired and still sore from my bruises, but the teas Simba made me seemed to help. The prospect of going home gave me the strength to keep walking.

By mid-morning we came into what must be their base camp. A field kitchen was set up. Roasting over the fire on a spit was some kind of animal about the size of a pig. The cook gathered the juices that ran off the carcass and spooned it over the meat as he turned the spit. The smell of that roast made my stomach growl. It'd been many hours since we last ate, and then it was only some fresh fruit, dried meat and some sort of bread that was dry and chewy. This meal smelled wonderful!

There were several big trucks parked off to one side of the fire, and behind them were several large cages. The cages appeared to be empty. A dozen or more tribesmen were busy tying tarps over the truck beds. The weight on the trucks shifted back and forth as the tarps were secured. I could hear the sounds of stressed animals screaming with fear and anger. Some of the sounds I couldn't identify, but I'm sure there were large cats of some kind in there.

I could see the airplane parts on one of the trucks which reminded me again of what we had survived. Thankfully, they were covering that load with a tarp as well.

One of the trucks parked farther away didn't move around as much as the others, and it almost sounded like people crying. I couldn't be sure and decided it would do no good to investigate. Jake and I went to the camp kitchen hoping they would feed us.

Just seeing the trucks made me want to cry. I blamed my tears on the smoke from the fire, but I knew Jake was as relieved as I was to see motorized transportation in front of us. We were tired of walking, and I was elated to think the hard part of the trip was over. These trucks would be our ride to the town where we would catch a ship to take us home.

The cook sliced some meat off the spit and poured thick gravy over it, handing a bowl to me and one to Jake. It tasted so good; I ate it all.

The men who rescued us shouted orders to the natives and later came to the fire for their meal. There was a big coffeepot off to the side of the fire. I didn't know if it had coffee in it or tea, but I could see the liquid was dark when Marcel poured some in a tin cup. Whatever it was, he didn't offer me any, so it must not have been Simba's tea.

"We'll finish loading the truck and head out this evening after dark," Marcel told us. "It's cooler then." He added under his breath, "and with fewer eyes to watch us."

A place was cleared in back of the truck with the airplane parts for Jake and me to sit with Simba and Kibwe. There was a brief but loud discussion between Marcel and Gus. I don't know what they said to each other, but it didn't sound good. Gus walked away in a huff and gave me a sideways sneer. Whatever it was about, Gus was not happy with the results.

It was much nicer traveling in the cool of the evening. I was happy to be riding out of this place; the sooner, the better.

"It's sure nice to sit, even in the back of a stinky, dusty truck," Jake said. "I was tired of walking. What do you think are in those cages?"

"I don't know, and I'm not sure I want to know."

The miles sped by, but the ride was far from smooth. Dust rolled up inside the truck bed where we sat. It was hard to believe it was this dry when it had rained so much a few days earlier. Any attempt at conversation was thwarted by the noise and dust that filled our noses, eyes, and mouths if we tried to speak.

We drove all night and most of the next day, with only a quick break for food and to relieve ourselves. The trucks finally stopped next to a warehouse on the outskirts of the first town we had seen in a long time. Gus and Marcel gave instructions to Simba and Kibwe and then led Jake and me to a hut where we could rest. Simba gave me a sideways glance before he left. The look made me nervous, but I figured I didn't have to be around these strange men much longer. By tomorrow we would be out of here.

There were two canvas cots in the corner of the hut. I set my pack under one of them and crawled onto the bed, hot, tired, and relieved to be back near civilization again.

The excitement of being in a town was more than Jake could stand. He kept pacing and looking out the hut doorway. "We're going home! We're going home, Kelly!" Jake kept saying. "Aren't you excited?"

"Yeah, I wonder how long it will take to get home," I replied, with concern in my voice. "But it doesn't matter—anything will be better than where we've been."

Gus came to our hut a little later with some dinner for us. "You kids stay put. Don't go wandering into town, there are some unscrupulous men here, and you don't want to get kidnapped or anything. Marcel is arranging for your passage on the ship. We wouldn't want you to get lost, now would we?" he asked with a gleam in his eye.

Jake wanted to go exploring but paid heed to the warning from Gus. "No, I certainly don't want to get kidnapped," he said.

"I wonder why we can't go to town with one of the guides," I said. "It would sure be nice to see civilization again."

As night settled in, Simba came quietly into our hut. His movements were almost cat-like as he approached my cot. "Tea for girl," he said as he handed a strange carved wooden cup to me. "Only for you," he added. Then just before he slipped into the darkness, he added in a whisper, "Listen to your spirit."

I figured it was more tea to make me strong, and I gratefully sipped the strange tasting warm liquid, but

I was puzzled by his statement if I'd heard it right.

Listen to my spirit? I wonder what he meant by that? I drifted off to sleep.

"You called me?" the voice said. There standing before me was the leopard I had seen that night in the jungle just before we were rescued. I was surprised to see him here in the city. Surely someone would shoot him if they saw him. I didn't know if the leopard was male or female, but by the way he "spoke" to me, I assumed he was male.

"I, I don't think so." I stammered. "I don't remember calling you. What do you want?"

Once again the leopard just stared at me and waved his long tail in the dirt.

Why is he just looking at me and not answering my question? I remembered the dream I had before and thought it odd that I was dreaming about this wild animal again. He wants me to ask him something, I guess. So I said. "I don't know what I should ask you. We have been rescued and will be going home soon. I don't know what else to ask."

The leopard said, "Trust your intuition. Do not trust what you think you see, but listen inside. Go to the docks and see for yourself."

"I was told there are bad men in the city and I should stay here," I responded.

"There are bad men everywhere, and you must see the dangers," he purred. The leopard came close to me, so close I could feel his silky smooth coat. "I will show you," he replied. "Climb onto my back."

In an ordinary world, if a wild jungle animal, especially a dangerous leopard, had approached me I would have been frightened; and to even imagine one would communicate with me was totally out of this world. His thoughts were like words, and I understood everything he said. It should have felt odd to get on his back, but for some reason, it seemed as natural as climbing on a pony's back except for the ripple of his tight muscles and his soft sleek skin. He walked so quietly, no one noticed us leave the hut. The leopard ran down the streets so fast, no one in the city saw him. Occasionally a native bringing in trade goods looked up and waved. Only a few people could see.

"Where are you taking me?" I asked.

"You will see," was the only reply I got until he stopped close to the loading docks.

"Look there," he demanded.

There was a big wooden platform, like a stage, and waiting alongside the stage was a line of young African boys and girls. Their faces looked sad. Some of them were crying.

"What is going on?" I asked.

"Look," the leopard answered.

I watched as the children climbed the steps one at a time and stood on the stage. One man looked inside their mouths and turned them around to look them over carefully. The crowd of men below the stage shouted things that I didn't understand, and when they were quiet, one child left the stage, and another stepped up as the man prodded them. It looked like they were moving cattle to slaughter.

In the distance, I saw a cage where some of the children were made to wait. There were three different pens in the area; each was surrounded by bars. I saw some of the children reach out to someone as they passed by and heard them cry as they went to a different pen.

"Are they selling children?" I asked in amazement.

"Yes," the leopard growled.

"Those poor kids!" I gasped. "What about their parents?" The leopard did not reply. "Why are you showing me this?" I cried.

"You must know what is going on here," was his only answer.

"No, first you must tell me. Why are you showing me this?" I demanded. "Are you telling me this is what they'll do to us? They're going to sell us as slaves?"

"The boy is strong and would bring good money on the block, but a young white girl would be worth more to these men."

"We are going to be sold? But how is that possible?"

"You have already been sold," he said.

"Sold! Sold? We have been sold? Who sold us and to whom?" I shouted.

The leopard didn't answer. He just turned and headed back to the hut.

"What should we do?" I asked in a panic.

"Trust in your spirit," the leopard said. "Sometimes the things you think are good are not, and sometimes the things you think are bad are for your own good."

Chapter 6

I woke up gasping for air. Sweat ran down my face, and my heart beat fast as I looked around the hut. It was still dark, and Jake was asleep next to me. My dream seemed real but impossible to believe. Who'd believe a leopard took me for a ride through the village and to the docks without anyone seeing us? I must be crazy to think we would be sold as slaves.

I shook my brother on the shoulder to wake him. "Jake," I said in a whisper. "Jake," I repeated. "Wake up. I just had a terrible dream. We have to leave."

Sleepily Jake stretched. "Is it time to get on the ship?"

"No time to explain. We must leave right now!" The tone of my voice must have alerted Jake because he sat up, instantly awake.

"No, no we can't leave—this is our only chance to go home," Jake pleaded. "We are so close—what you're saying makes no sense."

I had to admit that Jake was right. It made no sense to leave when we were so close to going home. Funny, though, neither Gus nor Marcel asked where we lived. I don't remember telling either of them where we needed to go. How will they know which ship to put us on?

"I don't want to go back out there alone. Where would we go and how would we survive? I'd rather take our chances on the ship." Jake said.

"I don't know, I had this dream about them selling slaves," I tried to explain.

"Slaves?" Jake shouted, "Don't be silly; no one buys slaves anymore."

It was clear that my brother didn't believe me and wouldn't leave. I couldn't bear to think about what would happen if I left him alone. It was starting to get light outside, and my night's vision about riding a leopard to the docks seemed like only a silly dream now.

"Maybe you're right," I said with little conviction. I was uneasy about our decision to stay but more concerned about what would happen to us in this strange city.

"Wake up kids," a deep voice bellowed through the doorway. It was Gus. "Gather your things. It's time to go."

Jake was up in a flash. He put on his sandals and grabbed his bag. "Hurry, let's go," he whispered. "We'll be right there," he shouted back to Gus.

I sensed my brother's excitement and couldn't help but feel a twinge of anticipation in the pit of my stomach. The desire to go home clouded over any apprehensions I had earlier.

"Will they feed us on the ship?" Jake asked as Gus led us to a truck outside the hut. All he got in reply was a grunt as he slid across the seat next to the driver who was already behind the wheel. I climbed in next. Gus closed the door. He said something to the driver in a language I didn't understand, and the truck sped off, spewing dust behind us.

Chapter 7

The port was large compared to the small villages we'd seen, but it was not a thriving city. Most of the homes were little more than shacks with thatched roofs. Almost all of them had holes in the chinking, and the paint had long since faded, leaving only the color of sand. The traffic was a combination of trucks, automobiles, and donkeys carrying heavy burdens on their backs. The closer we got to the city center the more decayed it seemed, except for a few large cars and nice buildings here and there. It was hot and dry. I was hungry and thirsty but decided not to ask the driver for anything. We should be on the ship soon.

We seemed to be taking all the back roads. It was odd to be driving close to the loading docks and not the passenger ramps. Jake looked over at me. I was sitting stiff, my eyes were opened wide, and my face felt hot.

"What's the matter, Sis?" Jake asked. "Are you sick again?"

"Oh, Jake," I said, "I think we're in trouble."

"What do you mean?" He almost cried.

The driver stopped at a building next to the dock. Jake and I got out, and standing before us was a stocky, black man with a deep scar on his face. The driver threw our packs on the ground near our feet then took off like something was after him. The big black man motioned for us to follow him into a structure.

"Well, it's not a luxury liner but as long as it gets us out of here..." Jake started to say.

"Oh, Jake, I don't like this." Beyond the small building, I could see a flat cargo ship and shook my head. No other words escaped my mouth.

The ship's horn blasted, signaling it was about to get underway.

"Hapa! Haraka! Haraka!" the man shouted in Swahili. "Here! Hurry; hurry!"

I felt blinded from the bright sunlight outside as we were pushed through a dark hallway and then a small room. The door closed behind us, and the sound of metal on metal made an eerie sound.

"I think they just locked us in here." Jake shouted, "Help! Help! Let us out of here!"

I thought I was going to pass out. I had been holding my breath since I first saw the ship, and now my breathing was shallow as the realization of what was happening slowly registered.

As my eyes gradually adjusted to the minimal

light that filtered in through slats at the top, I could see this room was a rectangular wooden crate. At one end of the container was a bunk bed with a large box next to it. At the opposite end was a curtain hiding what I discovered to be a chemical toilet.

Before long, the rumble and squeak of some kind of large machinery drew close, and our tiny room was lifted off the ground.

"I...I can't believe this. They put us in a cage like animals!" Jake spat furiously. "This looks like one of those crates they used for hauling wild animals to zoos. I saw a movie one time where they used these big cranes at the dock to load cargo on the ships. I think that's what they're doing with us. Why are they doing this?"

We could hear a lion's roar and what sounded like an elephant trumpeting in distress.

"These people are poaching animals," I said. "And us!"

"What are you talking about?" Jake's voice quivered as he stared at me.

"Remember I told you about the dream where I saw kids being sold as slaves? We were sold, too. We were sold, Jake, as slaves."

"That's plumb crazy, Sis. I remember you told me your dream. I thought you were nuts. Who would sell us? Who would buy us? We're Americans—no one can sell us; we're free. And besides, who still buys slaves these days? It's illegal!"

"Well, how do you explain all this?" I said waving my arms around the container.

I could tell Jake was furious. He kicked the bed by the wall and stomped around the small, dimly lit room, kicking anything he saw. He looked around in a panic then looked up at the slats on top.

"I wonder if we stood on the top bunk if we could reach those slats and escape," he said.

I didn't respond. The horror of being locked in this small container would be overwhelming if I allowed my fears to get the best of me. I never had claustrophobia before, but I fought against the fear now.

I kept thinking about the ride the leopard gave me to the docks where the native children were being sold at auction. That could have been us! In my dream, I saw children that were pushed up on a stage, and it looked like men were bidding on them. I don't know how we were sold since we didn't go on the stage. It was difficult to think clearly with all that had been happening.

"At least, for now, we're safe," I said more to myself than to Jake.

"The slats are too high to reach anyway," Jake sighed.

It was hot. Hardly any air circulated through the

crate. I went to the bunk to lie down.

"You don't mind if I sleep on the bottom bed, do you? I just want to fall asleep and never wake up." I sighed and was asleep before Jake answered.

Later that afternoon, after the sun had sunk low in the sky and the temperatures dropped to a bearable degree, I got up to relieve myself behind the curtain. Jake was starting to wake up from his sleep when I went to the box next to the beds and looked inside.

There was an insulated crock of water. Next to it were two ceramic cups, a paper bag with dried bananas and mangoes, two long loaves of bread, two small plastic jars with something like nut butter in one and a dark fruity spread in the other. There was a wooden knife for the spread. Wrapped in gauze was a long cylindrical roll that looked like a sausage of some sort. The box was the only other piece of furniture—if you could call it that—in the room.

I filled the cups with water and made two sandwiches with the bread and the spreads. This time I had to consider my strength and would eat, even though I was not hungry.

"Here, Jake, you'd better eat. Who knows when we will get the chance again."

We ate the sandwiches in silence trying to make sense of what was happening.

"I should've listened to you when you wanted to

leave during the night," Jake finally admitted. "It's my fault we're in this fix."

"No one's to blame, Jake. What's done is done, and there's nothing we can do about it." I had heard rumors about what could happen to young girls who were kidnapped. They were made to be prostitutes, and I was not certain I could survive something like that.

"Let's try some of that sausage or whatever it is. I'm still hungry," Jake said.

"We may have to bite into it," I said. "They didn't leave a knife sharp enough to cut it."

"Wait," Jake said reaching into the front pocket of his shorts. "I almost forgot! I still have the pocket-knife Dad gave me on my last birthday."

"Oh! I think today is my birthday," I remembered. "I wonder if I still have the present Mom was saving for me." I grabbed my backpack and looked inside the main compartment. "It's still here!" I said. "It's a little wrinkled, but it still has the bow on it."

"Open it!" Jake said. "We'll celebrate your birthday right now. Open it so we can see what she got you!"

It was too dark to see the colors of the silky material, but I remembered it had a purple ribbon tied around it in a bow. "Good thing Mom wrapped it in material and not paper, or it might not have survived all that rain in the jungle," I said. "She must have known to use something sturdy." I paused, thinking. "No," I finally said, "I don't want to open it yet. I want to keep it just like it is. It still has Mom's touch on it." It felt good just to hold it in my hands. "It's like I'm still connected to her."

Chapter 8

We made the best of our time stuck together in that stuffy container. Now and then I could hear someone whistling a tune in the distance. Jake hollered for them to help us the first few times, but no one ever came. The animals seemed to quiet down. I imagine they resigned to their fate or were too afraid to make more noises.

We slept as much as we could, which made it difficult to keep track of the days and nights we were on the ship. But we also had plenty of time to talk.

"I'm starting to forget a lot of things, Sis," Jake said. "Tell me some stories about when we were still living in Florida."

We talked about our camping trips and the trips to the beach where we body surfed on the waves.

"One wave was so big it tumbled you over and over in the water. I thought you were going to drown!" I laughed. "Mom always said, 'don't ever turn your back to the ocean: that's when the big ones come and catch you off guard,' and that's what happened. It just swept you off your feet."

"Yeah, I remember that," Jake said. "It wasn't fun at the time. My belly got scraped on the sand, and I swallowed a lot of salt water, but I kept going back to catch another wave. That part was fun."

We talked about school and our friends. I tried to think of everything to tell him—the funny stuff, the sad stuff, like when my goldfish died, and about the black cat that showed up at Halloween one time; we named her Spook.

The pain of all we'd lost was still fresh in our hearts but having each other to share the tears helped us to grieve and allowed us the chance to heal a little.

I told Jake more about my last dream with the leopard, and I described the thrill of riding on his back as he ran through the streets.

"That must have been wonderful. I wish I had a leopard or something that would come to me in my dreams. I wonder why I don't have a spirit animal watching over me, too."

"Spirit animal?" I had never thought about the leopard being a spirit animal. "I wonder if that is why he told me to *listen to my spirit*." I tried to recall exactly what the leopard said. Then I remembered it was Simba who first told me to listen to my spirit! What did Simba know about the leopard? For some questions, there were no answers. I decided I would try to listen for the spirit to guide me.

"If we ever go home, Sis," Jake asked wistfully, "what do you want to be when you grow up?"

"What do you mean 'if?'" I demanded. "We will go home—we will!" The anger and determination in my voice must have given Jake some hope.

"Okay, then, what will you be when you grow up?" he asked again.

I thought about how to answer. "I always thought I'd like to be a doctor like Dad, but not one of those doctors that travel to foreign countries."

"But we're in a foreign country now," Jake said.

"I know, how could I forget? I feel so bad for those animals in the cages and those poor kids! There has to be some way to stop those men from doing this."

I thought for a few minutes about what could be done. Maybe if we told the port authorities when we got to where we were going, they would check into it. Maybe someone there could help us get home. It just seemed so hopeless right now. Whoever put us in this cage would certainly not let us talk to anyone official. They must all be in on this.

To change the subject I asked, "What do you want to be when you grow up?"

"I don't know....I think about it sometimes, but it just doesn't seem like I'll ever grow up. Who knows what will happen to us when we get out of here?" Jake added, "You really think we'll get home?"

"Well, I know I will; I can't say for you." The thought of leaving without Jake made me ashamed to even consider it, so I added, "We will both go back, I just don't know to where."

"What do you mean?" Jake asked.

"Well, we could probably go stay with Aunt Emma. I don't know who else would take us," I said.

"I don't want to stay there," Jake replied as he wrinkled his nose. "I like Aunt Emma and all, but she and Uncle Will smoke too much. I can't stand the smell of their house."

Something changed the feel of the ship's movement.

"Hey, what was that?" Jake asked. The ship's horn blew one long blast then three short ones. "I think we're getting ready to land. Do you think we're finally getting off this ship?"

We had heard other horn blasts during the trip, but this is the first time it felt like the ship was slowing down.

"I wonder where we are and what will happen to us here!" Jake said as his voice cracked, holding back tears.

Chapter 9

After the ship docked, it seemed like hours before we felt any movement. Jake listened intently for sounds of nearby people so he could shout to someone—anyone—to rescue us. There were lots of loud engine noises. I guessed they had some kind of machinery to unload all the cargo.

"What is that?" Jake asked. "We're swaying."

"It feels like a crane is picking up our container again," I said. "Now, what's that?"

"It sounds like a truck. They must have put us on a truck. Help! Help!" Jake cried, but his shouts were not heard over the sputtering of the truck engine and rattling of the container. As we bounced over the uneven ground, light poured through the top slats, and we could see blue sky for the first time in a long time. The air was still hot and sticky, but it was fresh with a slight breeze now that we were away from the ship's other cargo containers.

Eventually, the truck stopped, and we heard several men's voices as they came closer to the container. Jake was ready to shout for help again, but before he could holler, a voice with a French accent shouted up to us. "*Bonjour*. Are you two okay in there?"

"Help, let us out of here!" Jake shouted. "Someone kidnapped us and put us in here. Get us out. Please!"

In minutes, the chains rattled, and the metal lock broke open. A tall black man opened the container, wrinkled his nose and stepped back.

I hadn't noticed the stink of stale body sweat, fear, and the foul odor from the chemical toilet while in the container, but now, with fresh air in my face, I almost vomited from the disgusting smell. I had forgotten the sweet smell of fresh air.

It was hot and humid, and the brightness of the sunshine caused me to squint. Before us, stood a tall white man dressed in a tan suit that looked expensive and perfectly tailored. He had several diamond rings on his fingers. His neatly trimmed hair had once been black but now had streaks of gray just above his ears. He seemed to be inspecting Jake and me as he looked us up and down. Behind him was a large black car.

"*Bonjour*," the tall man said again, as we stood there staring at him.

"Thank you for rescuing us, sir," I said. "My name is Kelly Connor, and this is my brother, Jake. We were lost in the jungle when..."

"*Un minute s'il vous plaît*," the man said with a

gesture of his hand to halt the conversation. "You do not seem to understand. I just bought you. You will come with me to South Africa and work for me. I am afraid you have no choice in this matter."

"What are you talking about?" Jake shouted. "Are you crazy? We are Americans. You can't buy us like slaves—it's illegal to sell children."

"Oh, Americans are you?" the man asked. "Well, that is different then."

Jake looked over at me with his eyes wide in expectation as I said, "Yes, we are both from Florida and our parents—"

"Prove yourself to me," the man broke in, "If you are Americans, let me see your passports."

I had grabbed my bag before we stepped out of the container and remembered I had packed our passports before we left the plane the first time, right after the crash. I searched frantically through my bag and then grabbed Jake's backpack.

"They're not here!" I cried. "We had them. You have to believe us. Someone must have taken them! Honest! We had them—mister...ah... mister?"

"*Pardon moi*," the French man spoke. "*Je suis, Monsieur* Cleome. If you have no passports, then you belong to me. I paid a lot of money for you both. If you two behave yourselves, life may not be so bad with me."

I didn't like the way this strange man looked at me.

"You, *mademoiselle,* do not look like you have reached puberty and life would have been much worse than living with me," he said.

I was in shock at what the man said. Reference to my undeveloped body made me uncomfortable, and the insinuation about what could have been my fate made me feel sick. My eyes stung with tears, and I was about to faint.

Jake grabbed me by the arm and said, "Kelly, Kelly—are you okay?"

The nudge on my arm brought me back to my senses. I'd been holding my breath without realizing it, and now gasped for air. I could smell the foul odor from the container where we'd been imprisoned. That nauseated me, but I turned my head and took another breath.

"Mr. Cleome," I stammered, "we're very confused and don't understand what's happening to us. We were told that we would catch a ship to take us home."

"And that, my dear, is precisely what is happening. You have no passports—you now belong to me. When we get to Johannesburg, you will be taken to my home. Until then you must be quiet and not draw attention to yourselves." He added, "You are lucky I

76

am the one who bought you."

"Lucky? Lucky?" Jake said. "How can you possibly say that? We were sold as slaves and put in a box?"

"*Excusez-moi, s'il vous plaît,* I am so sorry for this inconvenience," Mr. Cleome continued.

"Inconvenience?" Jake yelled. "Inconvenience?" Then to me, he said, "What does he think this is? A picnic with ants?"

I said nothing. I just wanted this nightmare to end.

"We will stay here long enough for you to bathe and eat. I imagine the food in the box sustained you but brought little enjoyment."

"Enjoyment? Inconvenience?" Jake raged. "We were put in a cage like animals, fed dry food, warm water, and had to crap in a pot, and you call that an inconvenience? Mr...Mr. whatever your name is."

"I am terribly sorry for your—ah, discomfort" Mr. Cleome continued, "but there was no choice. I will explain it to you after your refreshment."

For the first time since we were let out of the container, I looked around us. Squinting against the bright sunlight, I saw a small primitive structure surrounded by palm trees and a few fruit trees of some type that must have been planted many years ago. The fruit looked ripe and ready to pick. The shack was not elaborate, but it appeared to have electricity. Beyond that were several shanties made of plywood and corrugated aluminum, probably someone's home and storage shed.

The wealthy man turned to us and said, "Please go inside and refresh yourselves."

Inside the main building, a table was filled with fresh fruit, a variety of vegetables, milk, juice, cereal, and hard boiled eggs. A small white refrigerator hummed on one side of the room, a desk and chair sat by the window. The doorway in front of us led into several smaller rooms where I discovered two shower stalls.

"Jake, look! They have showers!"

"It's the food I want!"

"Please, Jake, let's shower first. We both stink."

"Oh, OK sis, but I'm really hungry."

"I'm sure the food is there for us, but I can't stand myself any longer and just have to get rid of the smell from that container."

A table held two clean towels and two small bars of soap. Next to these were a couple of brightly colored shirts and baggy shorts of similar sizes rather like a one-size-fits-all style. I picked the one on top. They didn't seem to be boy or girl clothes but were clean and welcome after the soiled clothes we were wearing.

When was the last time we had clean clothes? I thought, then remembered, *oh, yeah, at the plane crash site. That was the last time we ...* I didn't finish the thought.

The water in the shower was not hot or cold—it was just warm—and felt wonderful. Mud ran off my body in streaks. I just stood under the shower enjoying the feel of the water cascading on me. This was my first shower in...who remembers how long, a month—six weeks maybe? I didn't know, and I didn't care at the moment. It was so refreshing. The soap smelled like coconut butter as I washed my hair. Next to the shower head, I found a comb that looked like it was made from coconut shells. I couldn't remember when I last combed my hair—or when I had clean hair to comb.

Sometimes the small things in life are better appreciated when you've had to survive without them.

I put on the red, yellow, and orange print shirt and the tan pants that had a draw string at the waist. It felt great to have clean, loose-fitting clothes. Jake had finished his shower before me and was in the other room. He had on a blue, green, and yellow shirt with the same design and similar tan pants as I wore. He was sampling the food on the table as he filled a wooden plate.

"Did you enjoy that shower as much as I did?" I

asked.

"I did, but not as long as you! I didn't want to waste any time," he mumbled with his mouth full. "Food is good—juice in the fridge. I didn't realize how hungry I was until I saw the food."

I went to the refrigerator to see what there was to drink. There were glass bottles of papaya juice and plastic bottles of water. I selected a bottle of juice and drank it while standing there with the door open.

"Remember what Mom used to say?" Jake said. "Get what you need out of the refrigerator and close the door. You're wasting the cool." Jake fell silent and stopped eating for a moment. The thought of our mother made both of us pause.

"That seems so long ago," I replied.

"I sure miss her," Jake finally said.

"Me, too," I said softly.

"I'm starting to forget what she looked like," he said.

The memory of our mother was starting to fade in my mind too, and this made me feel sad, lonely, and lost. "It's been so long since we were with Mom and Dad." A tear ran down my face, and I wiped it away with the back of my hand.

When we had eaten as much as we could hold, we wandered out the door into the light. Mr. Cleome was sitting in the shade of a palm tree waiting for us.

"I trust you found plenty to eat, *n'est-ce pas?*" he asked.

I was still worried about our future. We couldn't trust anyone, but it was nice to be treated with kindness. "Yes, thank you. It's been a very long time since we've had a shower. The dried food in the container was terrible, so we both really enjoyed the fresh food."

"*Très bien,*" Mr. Cleome said, "*Bon, Bon,* come, *mademoiselle, garcon,* it is a long journey still to where I live. We can talk on the way to the airplane *s'il vous plaît.*"

"Airplane? We have to get on another airplane?" My stomach turned, and I almost threw-up the meal I had just eaten. The thought of getting on another airplane terrified me. The nightmare of the crash in the jungle came jetting back to me. I looked over at Jake, and his expression showed the same horror I felt. My voice trembled "I, I don't know if we can get on another plane."

"*Oui, mademoiselle,*" Mr. Cleome responded. "*Pardon moi,* it is far to where I live, and I have a meeting to attend. I am afraid we must fly. It will be okay; I promise you."

Seeing we had little choice, Jake and I followed the strange Frenchman to his car and sat in the back seat with him.

The road was dusty, but the car was tight and had air conditioning. It was almost too cold, after spending so much time in the hot crate, but it felt good all the same. Jake was hugging himself for warmth.

I wanted to ask questions of this man who bought us, but my mind was too numb to think clearly.

We arrived at a small hangar at the end of a large airport. Apparently, many people owned private jets and kept them in this area away from the commercial airliners. Jake and I took our few belongings out of the car and entered the plane. It was much larger than the last one we were in—the one that crashed. This jet had two rows of seats facing each other with an aisle between them. Mr. Cleome went into the cockpit where the pilot was going through his pre-flight check.

Feeling a little apprehensive about flying again, I put my backpack in the overhead compartment and sat down. I motioned for Jake to sit next to me. We buckled our seat belts and took deep breaths. When we were cleared for takeoff, and the engine revved up, I grabbed Jake's hand. He squeezed mine so hard his knuckles turned white.

After the airplane was in the air and leveled off, Mr. Cleome came back and sat next to Jake.

"Let's get better acquainted," Mr. Cleome said. "I was only told your names and about the plane crash, but little else. Please tell me what happened."

"Our father is—I mean, was—a doctor, and he wanted to help the sick children here in Africa," I told him. "We were flying to the first village in Uganda when the plane crashed."

I told him we were from Florida and about my mother who was always searching for medicinal plants. As I talked, I wept, once again remembering the nightmare vividly.

No one spoke while I composed myself. I wiped my eyes with the back of my hand and continued, "So, now, how is it we ended up with you?"

"Well, *ma chère*, I am not sure what led you to me—or me to you, but here we are anyway," Mr. Cleome stated. "We will have plenty of time for explanations later on, but for now, allow me to explain a little about what I do. Maybe it will clear up some of the mystery for you, although it might create questions I cannot answer at this time.

"In parts of Africa, women and children are stolen from the jungle and savannas and taken to auction blocks. Traders bid on them and sell them as slaves. They are then shipped by containers, similar to what you were in," he told us. "But usually there are many people in one container and not much food. This is illegal of course, but they get away with it most of the time. I received a message from someone one evening that there were two white children for sale. The messenger told me where you would be, but I couldn't get there fast enough myself, so I sent a representative of mine to buy you."

"Gus and Marcel!" Jake shouted. "Those men who rescued us—sold us to you?"

"*Oui,* I am afraid that is true, *mes chéris,* they are scavengers and make a living doing whatever it takes to make money. They trap wild animals and sell them to zoos and private collectors all over the world. They kill elephants for the ivory, hides, and feet. They take anything that brings them money, dead or alive."

"And us?" I interrupted.

"*Oui,*" Mr. Cleome said. "For you, they received a lot of money for little effort."

"How much did they sell us for?" Jake wanted to know.

"That is of little concern for you, *mon garçon.*" Mr. Cleome replied.

"It's of big concern," Jake demanded. "We'll work and earn money to pay you back so we can go home!"

"I am afraid that is impossible," he said sadly. "For you see, without passports you cannot leave the country. And you have no birth certificates to obtain a passport. I am afraid you are stuck here. You belong to me, now."

I saw the anger well up in Jake. His face turned

beet red, and his eyes were wide with rage. He grabbed at his seat belt, unbuckled it and pushed himself out of his seat. He stomped his feet and clenched his fists and paced back and forth stuttering so much we could hardly understand what he was saying.

"Jake! Jake. Sit down," I pleaded. "Let's hear what else he has to say. We are stuck here and throwing a tantrum won't help." I turned to Mr. Cleome and asked with suspicion in my voice. "What do you intend to do with us?"

"My intentions are in your best interests," he answered. "You will understand more in time."

Jake plopped down in his seat, folded his arms, and fell silent.

"There's no hope of returning home, or to any of our relatives in the States," I whispered to Jake. "We are stuck here, like it or not. We should make the most of it and try to get along."

"I don't like it at all," Jake responded with contempt in his voice.

"It will not be so bad, I promise you," Mr. Cleome said. "I will expect you to do chores to pay your keep, and I expect you to get a fine education. Of this, there will be no argument."

Jake was ready to protest when Mr. Cleome continued, "I have rescued many children who were sold as slaves, and some of them still work for me even after they paid their debt from my purchase. With you being white children, I will explain that you are distant relatives recently orphaned and will now live with me."

Orphaned! That word was shocking. In truth, we were just that—orphans, but this was the first time I'd thought of us that way. I couldn't look at my brother because I knew we would both cry, and I felt like I was almost cried out. Orphaned in a strange, foreign country, what could be worse?

Chapter 10

Johannesburg, South Africa, was one of the largest cities Jake and I had ever seen.   It took us a long time to pass through the city and drive to the farm where Mr. Cleome lived. He told us he had several farms and raised many crops, including fruit, nuts, coffee, and sugar. He also raised sheep and cattle—not all on the same farm but in various places throughout South Africa.

Arriving at the mansion, I looked out the car window, and my mouth dropped open. I could only stare at the estate in front of us. The massive black iron gates swung open wide as the car arrived. The driveway curved around a central fountain with a flower garden circling it. A three-story chalk-white house stood atop a small incline, requiring a dozen steps or so to reach the porch and doorway to the house.

"It looks like a castle!" I gasped as I stared at the white columns on both sides of a gigantic doorway. There were many windows in long rows wrapping around the building. Dark green shutters were latched back and didn't look like they had moved in many years.

I was torn between being excited about living here and apprehensive about what work would be required from us to maintain it.

The butler opened the car door and spoke a friendly greeting in a different language than we had heard before. The smile on his face made it obvious he was genuinely pleased to have *Monsieur* Cleome home. He was courteous to us as we stepped out of the car and gaped at the huge building in front of us.

There were a dozen or so people lined up by the steps, all with smiles on their faces.

Mr. Cleome introduced his staff by name, explaining we were orphans from a distant relative of his, and he would now be raising us. This left little question as to why we were there.

A small framed woman with dark skin walked over to us and said, "Welcome, I am Eshe." I was grateful she introduced herself again since I had forgotten everyone's strange sounding names. It was hard to tell her age, but she had seen many years, and her eyes sparkled like stars. "I will show you to your rooms."

"The foyer opened into a massive receiving room with hardwood wainscoting gleaming from years of polishing. The faint scent of lemon oil was refreshing after all we had been through. Large heavy doors hid the secrets of what rooms were beyond them. One door stood open, and I could see into what was obviously a library with tall shelves filled with books of many colors. I thought it curious that was the only door open as if to welcome anyone inside.

There was a double staircase, with one side curving to the right and the other to the left to more rooms beyond. Hanging from the ceiling was a large crystal chandelier.

Eshe lead the way up the closest staircase.

"Miss Kelly, your room is here, and Master Jake will have the room next to yours." Eshe gestured. "Please forgive me for not having more time to prepare your rooms. The information we had was limited as to your likes and needs."

"This whole room is all mine?" I asked. "I have never seen a bedroom this large in my whole life!" The four poster bed had a sheer net draping on all sides, and when I asked about the nets, Eshe replied, "To keep out the bugs at night."

The room had a four-drawer dresser, a writing desk with a lamp, and a wooden straight back chair pushed under the desk, a velveteen lounging couch, and a stuffed chair with a floor lamp beside it. To the right was a private bathroom with a walk-in closet next to it. The closet was empty except for one dress on a wooden hanger.

"We will have to buy you clothes, but there is a wrap-around dress that should fit for now. You may want to put it on after you clean up for dinner."

Eshe prepared a light meal of fruit and sandwiches for us in the small dining room off the kitchen. When we were through eating, we went to our rooms. We had more to digest than food.

It had been a long time since I'd slept in a separate room from anyone else, and I felt a little lost to be alone now. I went to see Jake's room. It was a mirror image of my room, but it felt more like a boy's room than my own.

His closet was filled with shirts, pants, and a few jackets.

"Why do you suppose they shopped for you and not me?" I said.

"Too many questions, too few answers," Jake replied showing his sad resignation to our circumstances. "I don't want to think right now. I want to sleep for a week."

I noticed the dark circles under his eyes and realized I, too, was exhausted. I went to my room and had barely crawled between the sheets before I was fast asleep.

Morning came too quickly it seemed. I was trying to figure out where I was when someone knocked on my door. I sat up in bed like a snapped twig.

Eshe came in. "I know you are tired," she said.

"Everyone else has eaten breakfast, but we figured you and your brother needed rest, so I let you sleep in. After today you will be expected to get yourself up, dressed, and come to breakfast with Mr. Cleome. He likes to eat at 7:00 A.M. sharp when he is home."

The realization about where I was and what had happened to us was starting to sink in. I looked around the room for something familiar to focus on. Nothing of my old life could be seen. Neither my old clothes nor my pack. "My pack!" I exclaimed, "Where's my pack?"

"Eshe?" I hollered. "Eshe?" I was frantic. The last gift I would ever receive from my mother was in that pack. I had to find it. I had to!

"Do not worry little one," Eshe said as she came back into the room. "Your pack was too dirty and too worn out to salvage, but I put everything you had inside in the top drawer of the dresser, except the clothes which I took out and washed. They should be dry by now. I will go see."

I ran to the dresser and yanked open the drawer in panic. The few items I had carried seemed to be worthless now and out of place. The dried fruit and jerky made my stomach turn as I remembered how long we had survived on such meager rations. My butterfly hair clips were still there, next to the flint and fire starter kit.

91

The most precious item in my whole world was still wrapped in the brightly colored material my mother had used for my birthday present. On closer inspection, I saw the material looked like a silk scarf. That would be typical for my mother to use a gift to wrap a gift. This small package was more precious to me than the whole room, the whole mansion, and all of Africa. Nothing could be as valuable to me as the last gift from my mother—nothing. Tears started to form in my eyes when Jake came into the room dressed in new clothing.

"Fits me perfectly," he said. "I don't know how they knew what clothes to buy. What do you have?"

My back had been turned to the door when Jake came in, so I quickly put the gift back in the drawer and closed it. "Oh, not much of anything, just a wrap-around dress. Eshe said we can go shopping later."

"It seems funny I have clothes and you don't," Jake said as he left to go find the kitchen.

I really didn't care much about why there were clothes for Jake and not for me. I was still concerned about our situation and was lost in thought as I showered and went downstairs.

No one was around, but the breakfast nook was filled with pastries, fruit, cooked eggs, and meat of some sort. Two plates were set on the table with fresh juice next to them. We sat and wolfed down the food.

The abundance we had now was quite a contrast to the scarcity of what we had survived on the last few weeks.

When we finally finished our meal, Eshe came in and explained a few house rules. "No shouting, no running in the house, and meals are served family style in the dining room three times a day. Breakfast is at seven A.M. Lunch is at one, and dinner is at seven P.M. You are expected to keep your rooms clean. There are supplies in the bathroom for you to use and a broom in each of your closets. You will do your own laundry once a week. I will show you the other chores you will be expected to do later. Today you can walk around and become familiar with the layout of the gardens and farm. You will help with harvest when the time comes."

"Oh, here is where the slave part comes in," Jake said with contempt in his voice.

Eshe looked startled by his remark.

"Jake!" I reprimanded, "That was rude. Eshe has been kind to us. You should apologize to her."

"I...I'm sorry," he stammered, embarrassed but not sincere in his apology.

Eshe told us, "I was the interpreter when a tall African man came to the door that night to tell Mr. Cleome about the white children in the jungle. I know you are not relatives, but I am the only other person in the household who knows the truth.

"Mr. Cleome expects everyone to work—no free meals," Eshe said. "Mr. Cleome bought me off the traders many years ago. He never treated me as a slave. He bought many others, too. He gives everyone a home if they want it and pays them for their work. He keeps a little from their wages to pay back what he calls their 'loan' and offers every one of us an education. He says, 'Everyone should have the opportunity to learn. The world is better off if we educate the people'.

"After everyone receives the basic education, Mr. Cleome leaves it up to each person to decide what he or she wants to study while they are working for him. When the so-called 'loan' is paid back—they can stay and work at full wage, or they can leave to pursue a career. Many people stay and think of him as their father. The people who leave go on to college to get a degree in the field that interests them. Some of the people have become doctors and have gone back to their tribes to help them with modern medicine."

It was easy to see how much Eshe loved and respected Mr. Cleome. So did the entire staff who greeted him that night. I thought about my father. He had been respected, too, by the doctors and nurses who worked with him. A wave of sadness swept through me, and I felt tears forming in my eyes.

"I had a father, and I don't plan to replace him with this man!" Jake spoke with bitterness in his voice.

The look on Eshe's face was a mixture of sadness and embarrassment.

"I was not suggesting he replace your father, Master Jake, but Mr. Cleome does deserve respect and appreciation. Worse things could have happened to you."

I was impressed by what Eshe said about everyone getting an education. She was right about not knowing what would have happened if Mr. Cleome hadn't bought us.

"What about the clothes in my closet?" Jake asked.

"You will soon see," Eshe said. "Mr. Cleome had a beautiful wife. He loved her very much. They were so happy when she told him she was pregnant. I've never seen him so happy."

"What happened?" I asked.

"The baby came into this world too early. Madam had problems during the birthing and died soon after the baby was born. The baby, named Jacques, had to stay in the hospital for a few weeks, and during that time Mr. Cleome decided he would spend every moment possible with his son as soon as he came home from the hospital.

When Jacques was old enough not to need a nursemaid, Mr. Cleome took him everywhere. He traveled a lot and wanted his son by his side."

Eshe looked over at Jake and said, "He was about your same age when he died."

"He died?" Jake said. "How could the son of such a wealthy man die?"

"There are some things money cannot buy," Eshe said sadly. "Mr. Cleome wanted Jacques to learn about all their farms, where they were located and how to treat the workers, 'Someday this will all be yours' he would tell his son, but malaria knows no race, wealth, or other boundaries. Jacques grew very sick one time when they were out in the jungle and died before they could get back to a modern hospital.

"It was difficult for Mr. Cleome to lose his wife, but when his son died, his grief burrowed deep inside him. It was almost more than he could stand. We were afraid he would die, too."

"What happened then?" I asked.

"I tried to visit him in his mind's sleep and give him reasons to live. Maybe he heard me. Eventually, he managed to wake up from his depression. That was several years ago."

"What do you mean; you visited him in his sleep?" I asked. There was something odd but familiar about what Eshe said. It reminded me about my dreams with the black leopard.

"Villagers understand the spirit world. The shamans and medicine women know how to speak to people in their sleep. This is how we heal our minds when we need a better thought or if we need help figuring something out. " Eshe looked at me as if she were seeing deep inside my soul. It was an eerie feeling, but somehow I felt I understood what she was saying. It felt like we shared a secret.

Eshe continued, "Thousands of our children in the villages have been orphaned by one disease or another and Mr. Cleome rescued many of them. He even started a foundation to support research into the infectious diseases that kill our people. His money helped to develop a vaccination for malaria—too late for his son, but he has helped save many lives because of it. But he misses having an heir."

Then she looked at Jake, "When Mr. Cleome heard about you, he knew he could never replace his son, but he wanted to give another child a chance. It was like a gift had been placed at his feet."

"So that explains why there were clothes in Jake's room," I said. "That was Jacques's room."

"Yes, little one," Eshe answered. "He could not throw away the clothes of his son. He has not used that room for anyone else—until now, for you, Jake."

Jake lowered his head. I could see he felt a little

embarrassed by the way he had been acting toward Eshe and Mr. Cleome.

"Thank you for explaining that to us," I said. "But I don't understand how he found out about us."

Eshe looked at us as if she were trying to decide if we were ready to hear this. She eventually said, "Spirit guides us."

Those words rang deep inside me. Where had I heard about this before?

Eshe continued to explain. "The slave traders are evil men. They stole many people from my small village in Uganda. I was one of them. Many of our people died in transport. I was lucky to survive and be bought by Mr. Cleome. He is known by a different name at the docks. If the traders knew he bought slaves to educate and free them, they would not sell to him anymore. The traders think my people are animals and do not deserve to have a free life. They think Mr. Cleome sells slaves to other countries because he buys so many. That is why you and your brother had to be treated as slaves in the beginning and put on the ship like slaves. If anyone knew you would be treated differently, they would have killed you."

"Kill us?" Jake's mouth dropped open, and his eyes widened in disbelief.

"Yes, if those men were suspicious of Mr. Cleome

as a slave buyer, they would have killed him and you both and dumped you in the river to protect their trade. That is why you had to be placed in the container. It was for your protection."

"But why would they kill us! That doesn't make any sense!" Jack shouted.

"No reason, other than jealousy or to protect their slave trade. They do the same thing with the animals they trap and sell. They make so much money, they don't care if a few die. Some die at the port of customs. If an agent get suspicious about what is in the shipment, the traders will abandon the crates and the animals die of thirst, starvation, and fear. They figure there are more animals out there to trap, and they don't want to risk their trade or imprisonment. They think the same about the people—there are always more to kidnap and sell."

"That's horrible!" Jake said. "They just let people die, too?"

"Yes, my little man, which is why you should be grateful for your gift of life. You may not be where you want to be, but you are where you need to be."

Jake was silent. I could see he was trying to grasp all that Eshe was telling us.

"So by allowing them to treat us like animals, he saved our lives," he finally said as he was starting to understand.

"Did you ever go back to your village?" I asked.

There was a long silence between my question and her answer.

"I longed to go back in the beginning. I cried myself to sleep many nights missing my family."

I nodded, knowing exactly what that felt like. "But after you paid back your slavery price to Mr. Cleome, couldn't you go back then?"

"Little Miss, you do not yet understand," Eshe said. "Mr. Cleome gave me a chance for a new life. He never treated me as a slave. He paid for my education, gave me a good home, took care of me, and gave me the opportunity to help many more people than I would have if I'd gone back to my village. When the city people moved into our area, they burned the forests and fields where we gathered the herbs and roots for our survival. They planted many other things to bring them money, and our people had to move farther back into the jungle just to survive. The intruders built big cities that brought sickness, and that sickness spread to my people. Many parents died, leaving their children behind. Those children were stolen and sold if they survived.

"Enough talk for now, my children. Let's get started with our day. I am to show you around and explain what I can to you. Mr. Cleome is a busy man, and we might not see him for a few days. The time he took from his work to bring you home caused him much delay."

Eshe showed us around the mansion and took us outside to the gardens. There was so much to see and understand about this new life.

That evening after dinner, Jake and I went outside to sit in the garden and talk. The sweet smells of the flowers and herbs made me feel happy for the first time in a very long time.

"She's right, Jake," I said. "We are lucky to be here."

"I'll do what I have to do to earn my freedom," he told me. "But as soon as that happens, I'm going back home to America, one way or another."

Chapter 11

Mr. Cleome was gone for over a week. He didn't say where he had been, and we didn't see any reason to ask. Like it or not, this was our home for now.

The work we had to do on the estate was harder some days than others. I didn't care about housework; I preferred to be outside, but I learned how to appreciate a job well done whether by me or someone else. Eshe said, "Not all jobs are easy, but all work is necessary."

Working in the gardens made me happier. "I loved seeing spouts pushing through the soil with those two little leaves, expecting to become something much bigger than its present self." Someone once said that in the heart of every acorn is a mighty oak tree. Sometimes I wondered what was growing inside my own heart...*What is it I am supposed to do.*

Eshe seemed to enjoy teaching me about herbs and healing, and I really enjoyed learning from her. If my mother were here, the two women would be saving the world, I have no doubt. But then again, if my mother had not died in the plane crash—I wouldn't be here studying with Eshe. There is never a complete explanation for why things happen as they do and maybe it isn't necessary to know, but it is necessary to be grateful for what does come into our lives and make the most of the opportunities.

Some days the chores were light, and some days our work took the entire day, depending on what was going on at the farm. I didn't do much of the farm work, but I did help with the house garden, weeding and hoeing and picking off bugs—ugh—which I did not like to do. Eshe said those bugs made a good protein feed for the chickens, so they went in a deep canister with a screen lid. As soon as the chickens saw that canister, they fluttered and clucked and followed us as we went farther away from the garden. They knew a treat would be in that can. When we dumped the canister, the chickens were right there to grab the bugs as soon as they were set free. I don't think one escaped those hens.

Jake was still a bit rebellious until the day he was invited to sit with Langa, one of the drivers in the big combine. Jake called it "the mother ship." I guess there is something about guys and big machinery. It wasn't long before Langa let him take over the controls, and in no time Jake was driving in the row crops even better than the crew. He was a natural when it came to working the fields and driving the big rigs. He seemed to really enjoy farming. I was happy he found something he could do and feel good about. Since we were stuck here, we both needed to find a way not simply to endure our situation but to find some reason for us to be here.

"Sis, it was so cool!" Jake told me one day. "You should see me drive that rig! Today Langa let me park the combine in the machine shed. He said it needs some maintenance. He gave me a new name, too. He calls me *Msizi*; he said that means helper."

"That's great Jake. Is that what we should call you now?"

"No, you can still call me Jake, but I like it when Langa calls me that. He's trying to teach me his language."

"I thought you didn't see any reason to learn another language," I teased him.

"This is different. Most everyone speaks English here, but there are a few new people who don't. I thought it would be cool to be able to speak to them."

It took me longer to find my place than it did Jake. He loved the machinery and talked for hours about the way he could park the rigs in the machine shed or make the big turns without crushing the crop. There must have been something intoxicating to him about the smell of freshly tilled soil, because he would come in at night with a big smile. The white of his teeth was in sharp contrast to his tanned and dirty face.

Depending on what was happening on the farm, he would often go back out after dinner and work until dark. On those late nights, he'd come in, take a shower and fall into bed.

Most days he woke himself without the alarm, but with the late nights he didn't trust himself to wake up, so he set his alarm just in case he needed it. I think I only heard it once. He seemed to know when it was morning even if it was still dark outside.

I loved working with Eshe in the garden, but I felt dissatisfied, until the day someone came running from the barn to tell Eshe about a cow having trouble calving. She asked me to come with her in case she needed help. That day changed my life forever.

It was obvious the cow was in distress. Her sides heaved with labored breath, and she was restlessly crying a low moo. This was the family's favorite milk cow, and Eshe went to work on her.

Eshe said as she rolled up her sleeve and palpated the cow, "It's breech."

I was shocked to see her grease up her arm with vegetable oil and insert it in the backside of that cow.

"Get some rope," Eshe hollered. "I'll have to push the calf back in farther, so I can find its back legs." Eshe worked hard and fast, lying on her side in the straw with her whole arm inside the cow. "There is one leg, quick tie one end of the rope around that ankle and hold it, so it doesn't slip back inside. I have to find the other leg. When I get that leg out we will have to tie it to the other end of the rope in a half clove hitch then we'll have to pull hard and fast, so the calf doesn't drown."

I learned in Girl Scouts about tying knots, so making a half clove hitch was easy, but I must have been holding my breath because I felt dizzy and almost passed out. I was worried and afraid. I did not want to pull a dead calf!

"Okay, now pull!" Eshe commanded.

It was a struggle, but we managed to get the calf to slide out onto the straw. Eshe removed the birthing sack from the calf's face and gave it mouth-to-mouth resuscitation as she massaged his body to get the blood circulating. The calf wiggled, and his sides heaved with the rhythm of the breath she was blowing into its nose.

The joy that flowed through me was electric. Eshe brought back to life a baby that would have surely died and taken its mother with it. I had never seen anything like it. I looked at Eshe, covered in blood, goo, and cow manure. Her face glistened with sweat, and her smile was so big her teeth shone like stars in that dark barn.

"It's good now," was all she said.

At that moment I was hooked. I found what I wanted to do. I wanted to work with animals and bring new life into this world.

There was plenty to do, too. The ranch hands tended to the breeding stock farther away from the main ranch, and the commercial livestock were grazing on another ranch a few miles away. The milk cows, milking goats, and chickens were fed close to the main barn for the family's use. I loved working with them all. No matter what their future destination was to be, for now, in my care, I would treat them with kindness and respect.

A year had gone by when one day Mr. Cleome called us into his den.

"*Mes chers*, come sit. I want to talk with you."

I wondered what he wanted. He rarely invited us into his study.

"I am happy you are enjoying the farm and ranch work. *C'est l'heure*—it is time I show you more of my plantation."

"There is more?" Jake asked.

"*Oui, oui mon jeune homme*. There is much more."

'We knew the place we had been working was only part of his farm and ranch operation, but we didn't realize to what extent. There was so much more for us to discover."

It was wonderful to get away and see more of the country. Jake still hadn't warmed up to Mr. Cleome, but when they talked about farming, he would open up a little. I could see how important this was to the older man. He would ask Jake questions if for no other reason than to hear him talk.

We eventually became familiar with each place, and once a month we would return, depending on what crop was ready to harvest or what new breeding stock came to the ranch. Eshe always packed a picnic lunch for these outings.

When we sat down to eat at noon, either under a tree or by a stream, Mr. Cleome started to explain more about his life in South Africa.

I enjoyed these outings more than anything else. It was interesting to see how different things grew in different areas, pretty much like Florida in some ways and vastly different in others.

Once I asked him about his son, but he didn't want to talk about it. So I asked him to tell us more about how he found out about us. He evaded that question too, so I just listened to the things he did want to talk about, which was mostly about his farms and ranches.

He told us about the different crops and harvest

times, which varied with the seasons. He had huge vineyards, and he grew chicory root, sorghum, and sunflower seeds. There were sections of land with apples, pears, plums, beans, grains, soybeans, and peanuts. Peanuts—my favorite crop.

I told Mr. Cleome about my grandmother's brother, Uncle Lester, and his wife Phyllis, who had a peanut farm in Florida. Every year after harvest, they'd have a big peanut boil. He'd fill a huge cauldron with green peanuts still in the hulls, lots of salt, and enough water to cover the peanuts, and then build a fire under the cauldron. It'd take almost all day to boil the peanuts until they were soft inside. All the relatives and neighbors would come for the big social event. The adults took turns stirring the pot and adding firewood as needed. Eating boiled peanuts someone said, is an acquired taste, but I loved them from day one.

"Bon! Bon, ma chérie!" He said, "Perhaps we will have a peanut boil this year after harvest."

I loved his enthusiasm for boiling peanuts, and I looked forward to it. It made me happy to think I might be starting something new in South Africa!

When it was time to harvest the peanuts, Mr. Cleome was true to his word by hosting a harvest party complete with a big pot of boiling peanuts. All the people from miles around came to enjoy the bounty.

It was not the same as I remembered as a kid, of course, but nevertheless, the soft, salty peanuts were still delicious.

"I think this may become our annual tradition," Mr. Cleome said after shelling and eating a big hand full of peanuts. "I've enjoyed eating them raw for years, but this is a new delicacy."

Eshe told me this was the first party Mr. Cleome had thrown since his wife died.

"You are good for him," she told me. "You and Master Jake bring life back to this house and to Mr. Cleome."

I guess I was so busy thinking about my own life that I didn't notice how we affected the people around us. I smiled to think of how much he enjoyed eating those boiled peanuts.

Chapter 12

The years seemed to fly by. We had private tutors for our academic studies and mentors who offered us many diverse experiences. Over time, we learned a little about silversmithing, gemology, lapidary, timber, agriculture, mechanics, business, economics, and finance. Not so much to be an expert in any of these fields but enough to see if we had any further interest in pursuing any of these careers.

We both took flying lessons, which neither of us enjoyed at first because of our one disastrous experience, but I had less aptitude in dealing with the gauges and controls than Jake. He was a glass that was never full when it came to learning new things related to machinery and equipment.

Jake's body started to fill out. He developed muscles and sported a deep tan. Healthier than I'd ever seen him, he didn't look like my little brother anymore.

My reflection in the mirror showed feminine maturity, too, in a different way. I was tan, of course, and my figure was becoming apparent. Eshe helped me through puberty a few years ago, and though I was still young, she said I have an old soul. She explained many things about her beliefs, and they made sense to me.

I was beginning to understand there is often a bigger reason somethings happen, than what we can comprehend at the time. I didn't like what happened to my parents, but I started to see there were other ways to think about life, death, and the hereafter.

I loved learning about the herbs in the gardens. Eshe showed me how to pick them and dry them, so they could be stored for later use. Most everything in the garden was good for one thing or another. If one plant was good for healing, she was careful to tell me about how to prepare and use it. She also told me about the plants that looked similar but had different effects. There were a few that Eshe said she grew because they benefited the bees, or were companion plants to the vegetables. A few she simply said were just "good for the spirit." Those usually had pretty flowers and smelled wonderful. She used some herbs for lactating cows with mastitis or for the chickens with their ailments. She had herbs for women having trouble with their pregnancies and for men who got injured with farm machinery.

I told her as much as I could remember about my mother and the herbs she used at home. But I was too young to take as much interest then as I did now.

Eshe told me she came from a long line of medicine women in her tribe. "My *bibi*—my grandmother—was a medicine woman as was her *bibi*. The knowledge was passed down from our ancestors. My mama was teaching me what she knew before I was stolen from the village, but much of our knowledge comes from the herb itself. The herb tells us what it can do."

I had never heard this before but really wanted to believe it. I didn't learn enough from my mother, so I was happy that Eshe was willing to teach me what she knew. I guessed it would be up to me to learn how to listen to the herbs.

Eshe seemed to enjoy teaching me about healing. She never had children of her own, but wanted to pass on her knowledge to someone.

"It's no good for knowledge to die with one person," she told me one time.

I had to agree since there was no way I could retrieve the knowledge from my mother. I felt like a sponge absorbing all I could from Eshe.

I asked her about the tribe where she once lived, but she was evasive.

"I do not usually talk about my old days," Eshe explained. "It was a different lifetime and of little use now, but it seems right to talk to you about healing. Maybe someday you can be a medicine woman."

The thought of me as a medicine woman, scantily dressed in a flowered sarong with feathers in my hair, just didn't fit with who I was now, but I had to admit it sounded fun and intriguing.

There are so many different realities in this world. I would never have thought about the many African tribes and the things they do to survive. My previous world was so isolated and protected in comparison.

In addition to working in the garden, I loved working with the livestock, especially when there were babies to watch as they played with each other. The lambs and calves were so pure and cute when they were still little. Not that I didn't like the mothers, but many times they didn't want people messing with their babies. I had to be careful, but I couldn't help thinking maybe with my early imprinting that the next generation of animals would be more tolerant of humans. It made sense to try.

I thought I knew where my life would take me until one evening at dinner, Mr. Cleome told us the following day we would take a long trip. I had no idea that trip would change my life.

At seventeen years of age, I thought I knew my path, but there was still much I didn't know. Maybe we never get so old we know everything.

"I have business I must attend to, and *je voudrais que vous les enfants de m'accompagner*. I would like you children to accompany me." Sometimes Mr. Cleome spoke in French to us, and sometimes he used perfect English. *"Vous devriez apprendre une autre langue.* You should learn another language." He would often say.

I was starting to understand French as well as English.

Jake had refused to speak anything foreign in the earlier years. "I won't need to speak French when I go back to America," he'd say. But I could see he was starting to enjoy speaking words other people didn't understand.

We were told to pack a small bag with our toiletries, a change of clothes and our safari boots. "Are we going on a safari?" Jake asked.

"Presque un safari. Almost a safari. *Vous verrez.* You will see," he said.

Most of the early crops had been harvested, and we were heading into autumn. It was not yet time to work cattle so our excursion would be a nice break from the work we'd been doing.

Work is really not the right word to use. It was physically challenging, and sometimes the hours were long, but time seemed to fly by with so much diversion to keep us occupied. I remembered my father used to say, "If you find something to do that you love, you will never have to work a day in your life." He was not the first person to say that, I am sure, but I know how much he loved being a doctor, even when he came home late at night, exhausted. By morning he was anxious to start the day again.

"Sometimes my job is not easy," he'd tell us, "and sometimes it is heartbreaking when I can't do anything to help someone, but I still have to do my best and be happy for the people I can help."

After breakfast, we packed the Land Rover with our small bags and the basket of food Eshe prepared for us. Mr. Cleome had a few trunks packed in the back, but we were so excited about this new adventure, we didn't think much about them.

"What is the plan for today?" Jake asked. He sounded just as excited as I felt.

"I have not shown you everything yet and think it is time you see something that is *cher pour moi,* dear to my heart," he explained. "You will understand more when we get there. But for now, remember the roads we are taking. Someday you may want to come back here without me."

I had kept a journal since shortly after we arrived at the mansion in Johannesburg. When Eshe took me to town to buy clothes that first day, I'd asked if I could go to a book store where I bought a couple of blank journals. In one journal I wrote my memories and my night time dreams and fears. In the other journal, each night I wrote about what happened that day. So now I carefully wrote down each new road we took and the directions we turned.

Hours drifted by, and the terrain changed. It was interesting to see how the trees and grasslands became less developed and wilder.

Mr. Cleome told us, "There are many, *Réserves d'animaux,* animal reserves in this part of Africa. Taking people on a safari is big business for some. But what you will see soon is different. We do not host many *les tourists;* we are more of a research facility and a rehab center."

"What do you research?" Jake asked. He sounded intrigued.

"We rescue animals that have been captured, abused, and separated from the only society they have known and try to give them back their heritage. We heal their physical wounds and give them life again, with as little interference from humans as possible. There are some animals who have suffered too much to be returned to the wild, so we try to socialize them while giving them as much freedom as we can. We look for the things that make them comfortable, whether it is certain foods, landscapes, or companion animals. We have discovered a lot of things that we didn't know were important to them.

"The animals who just can't survive in the wild and refuse to be socialized, we make available to zoos that follow our guidelines for making them comfortable in captivity—or as much at home as possible."

"You sell animals to a zoo?" Jake asked. "That doesn't sound right. How is that different from the men who poach them?"

"The difference is, we didn't take them from their environment. We rescued the animals who had been captured, beaten, and left to die. We give them a life that might not be as good as what they had but certainly better than they were getting."

It was mid-afternoon when we drove into a compound that had a guard at the gatehouse. The guard smiled and opened the gate when he saw Mr. Cleome. They exchanged greetings in what I assumed was a native language, and we drove a few more miles to a lodge built among the trees.

"Home away from home," Mr. Cleome said. "This is where we will sleep on this trip. It has all the creature comforts you'll need. I'll give you a quick tour, then we will eat and turn in early. Tomorrow will be a big day. Let's get up about 4:00 am. You have much to see."

I was so excited I could hardly sleep. I could hear many animals calling to each other in the night. Lions roared, and many mysterious sounds echoed through the night. It reminded me of the time Jake and I had been lost in the jungle after the plane crash, but this time I didn't feel frightened or alone. I had barely gotten to sleep when Mr. Cleome knocked at my door. "*Réveiller. Réveiller* you sleepy heads."

He didn't have to call me twice. I was up and dressed and out the door in a matter of minutes.

I could hear Jake rattling around in the room next to mine, and I knew he was up and ready to go too.

At breakfast, in addition to Mr. Cleome, his driver, Jake, and I, there were several gamekeepers. They each wore a dark green apron with a logo embroidered on the left chest that looked somewhat like a coat of arms, and their name was embroidered on the right side of the apron. That made it easier for me to remember their names when we were introduced. There were a couple of veterinarians in white jackets eating breakfast, and some whom I assumed were paying guests were filing in.

There were too many people in the dining area for us to meet them all. Mr. Cleome was busy visiting with many of them. I could see he really loved this place. His smile was radiant. When he laughed, I could see his perfectly formed teeth with a few gold fillings in the back. What I loved seeing the most were his eyes as they scanned the room, noticing everyone and their movements, but with crisp attention to the person to whom he was speaking. It was like he captured his audience with his words but allowed full attention to the room. I was starting to see another side of the man who had bought us.

"What's all this about?" Jake asked me when he finished his breakfast. "Why do you think he brought us here?"

"I don't know for sure, but he must have wanted us to see this for some reason. Look how everyone gathers around him. You'd think he owned the place or something."

"That's crazy. Who would own something this big—big enough to need a guard at the gate? It looks like one of the state parks in the southern part of Florida. Maybe bigger."

Before we could talk about it anymore, Mr. Cleome came over to where we sat and said, *"Prêts mes amis?* Are you ready to go? We have a big day ahead of us."

A jeep was waiting outside, and when the driver saw us, he got out and opened the back door for Jake and me to climb in. Mr. Cleome had already slid into the passenger seat but sat twisted half way around so he could talk to us.

"C'est mon endroit préféré. This is my favorite place in the whole world. I hope you enjoy the tour."

It was a little noisy and dusty, so we didn't talk

much on the trip. We drove for about a half hour before Mr. Cleome stopped and pointed to a series of buildings. "This is the veterinary clinic. Wounded animals are brought here to be treated. We won't go in there today; the animals are already frightened and stressed without having us to worry about. They had cruel treatment before they came here."

The road was not much more than two tracks in the grasses that seemed to stretch all the way across the grassland. We crossed a stream, and the terrain changed a little. We saw a few lions fanning themselves with their tails, lying in the shade of a squatty tree. Off in the distance, we could see several Zebras pawing in the dust.

"Why do the zebras graze over there when the lions are so close by?" Jake asked. "Don't they have to be worried about the lions eating them?"

Mr. Cleome laughed. "Sorry, Jake. I didn't mean

to laugh—that is a good question. The lions know not to kill everything or there would not be enough food later. Instinctively, they only kill when they are hungry, and they know which ones are old or injured; ones that would not survive in the wild. The lions? They are not hungry right now."

"Do we have to worry about being their next meal?" he asked a little nervously.

Again Mr. Cleome laughed. "If we were not in this jeep but walking around at night with a limp, then yes, maybe we would be in danger of being their next meal. But most of these lions have learned we are not here to hurt them but to help. They don't care so much about human flesh. There are much more tasty things out here to eat."

We saw many animals, including some I had never seen before with names I couldn't remember. At dinner that evening, we met again in the dining area with a few of the same people we saw at breakfast.

"Tomorrow, we will see the elephants!" Mr. Cleome told us. "After you eat, you might want to get some sleep. Morning will come soon."

I don't remember listening for the animal calls that night. It was still dark when I heard a knock on my door. Mr. Cleome was calling, "Réveiller, c'est le matin. It's morning."

I was excited to see the elephants. Every year when the circus came to our town in Orlando, I headed first to the elephant tent. I was amazed at how docile the elephants were and how easily they did their tricks for being such large animals. I used to dream about having an elephant of my own. Once I saw a special on television where an elephant would drag logs out of the forest. Sometimes it would pick up a smaller log with its trunk and stack it on a pile. I'm not sure why I thought this was what I wanted—but I'd been intrigued with the elephants ever since.

"Will we really get to see elephants in the wild today?" I asked.

"*Oui, oui,* we should be able to find them. They are in a large area, but my keepers keep track of where the herd is feeding. They roam quite a lot."

Half the day passed before we found the elephants. It was worth bouncing over the rutted road and eating dust just to see these majestic animals roaming free and nursing their young. It was beyond what I expected. They used their trunks like hands, feeling and petting their babies. They called them if they got too far away. When they went to the river, they'd scoop the water in their trunks and squirted it in their narrow mouths. Sometimes they sprayed their backs with water and walked out into the deeper pools. I couldn't believe animals that big could swim, but they did. I could have stayed there all day just watching them.

At dinner that night we were the last to the dining area to eat. Everyone else had finished their meal, and the tables were cleared, except for the plates that awaited us. I'm not sure I tasted anything. It was a long, wonderful day, and I was too tired to chew.

"You are quiet tonight, *mon amie*" Mr. Cleome said.

"I'm still thinking of those elephants. I can't believe anyone would kill them. They seem so gentle and trusting."

"*Oui,* it is hard to understand the greed in men. But don't make the mistake of believing elephants are gentle in the wild. They can be ferocious if they feel threatened."

We took two more day trips from our camp before we headed home. I really didn't want to leave, but Mr. Cleome promised to bring us back sometime.

"Next time we will visit a different section of the Reserve where you can see a variety of animals in different ecosystems."

It was difficult to imagine all the diversities, and I could hardly wait for our next outing!

Chapter 13

Our next trip came much faster than anyone could have predicted. One evening Jake and I went to the music room after dinner. We were expected to take music lessons along with our other studies, and while Jake never mastered an instrument, he had a voice that could make you sit on the edge of your chair and hold your breath, not wanting to miss a single note. I loved playing the piano, so when I played a tune, Jake would sing. Mr. Cleome enjoyed listening to us from the den, but he didn't have a good singing voice. We had to chuckle to ourselves when we heard him attempt a song. He didn't know we heard him, and we were careful to keep it a secret. There is no sense in telling someone they can't do something when they enjoy trying.

One evening we were engaged in our music when Mr. Cleome was called to the library to meet with a visitor. He often had business associates come over, and the library is where he greeted them so they could conduct business without being disturbed. We didn't pay much attention to how long he was gone.

We were too engrossed with our song.

Jake was the first to see Mr. Cleome enter the music room. He stopped singing as soon as he saw the expression on the older man's face. I looked up to see why Jake had stopped then followed his gaze to the doorway. Mr. Cleome stood there with fists clenched, the vessels on his neck protruded so far I was afraid he would pass out. I could sense energy spiking all around him. He hurried over and told us to sit on the couch next to him. We had never seen him so angry. It was frightening.

"I had an urgent message just now, and I need to talk to you both," he said. "Something has happened that I must attend to, and I need your help."

Jake and I looked at each other not knowing what to think. We had never been asked to help our benefactor before, and this was obviously gravely important by the way Mr. Cleome weighed his words carefully and spoke to us calmly but breathlessly. His face was flushed with anger, and he could hardly sit still, but the years of control allowed him to stay seated as he explained.

"There are a few containers of animals left on the dock that no one has taken possession of for several days. No one has fed the animals or given them water. I am afraid it is terribly ugly, but it is extremely urgent that I leave to see about rescuing as many as I can if any are indeed still alive."

This news sickened me—I had to swallow back the bile that filled my throat—I could not speak for fear of losing my dinner.

"What can we do?" Jake asked.

"I need you, Jake, to fly with me there. My pilot asked for a few days off, and I didn't see any reason why he couldn't leave. He would come back in a flash, but I'm afraid he is too far away. I must leave for the airport tonight, so I can fly out at morning's first light. I maintain an apartment near the airport. It will save us a lot of time driving tomorrow if we get there tonight. I could fly myself, but I need a copilot.

"I know you don't like to fly, but you have done well with your flying lessons. You have had more flight training than anyone else here. The time is urgent."

Mr. Cleome had urged Jake to learn to fly telling him, "You must face your fears, so they don't get bigger than you." Jake took the lessons because he didn't want to admit he was afraid, but he didn't find the joy in flying the skies that some pilots do. He liked the instrument panels and adeptly performed the simulated flights but preferred to stay on the ground.

"Tomorrow I need your help to rescue some animals." Mr. Cleome told him.

"Sure, whatever you need me to do," Jake said.

I knew his words did not match the dread he felt, but he was not going to admit to any weakness of his character.

"What can I do?" I asked.

"I cannot ask you to come with me, *ma chere* for the horror of what we may witness."

"But I want to help if I can do anything, anything at all," I pleaded.

"Oh, mes chers enfants, vous me faites très fier. You both make me proud. *Bien,* we leave for the airport in an hour. Pack lightly. I will have my plane fueled tonight so it will be ready to go first thing in the morning." Mr. Cleome often resorted to speaking French when he was deeply emotional—so I knew he appreciated our willingness to help.

The pre-dawn air was humid and sticky but the slight breeze was welcome. Jake and Mr. Cleome performed the preflight checks, and before long we were in the air. I was worried about what we would see when we arrived at our destination. Mr. Cleome waited until we were in the air to tell us the port where we were headed was the same one where he came to meet us all those many years ago. The nightmare we had faced then was coming back to life. But this time we were the rescuers instead of the captives. *There must be a lesson in here somewhere,* I thought.

"Please forgive me for not telling you everything earlier," Mr. Cleome shouted over the sound of the engines. "I didn't want you to worry about it. There is more to this story, but you will see what it is soon." I hadn't seen him this disturbed for as long as we had known him these last few years. *Seems like a lifetime...* my thoughts trailed off.

A car was waiting for us at the small airport in Bukoba. A few things had changed, but it was difficult to remember what it had been like when we were there before. When we made it to the dock, we could smell death, decay, and fecal matter before we saw what was waiting for us.

There were many people at the dock, shouting and rushing around, trying to get animals moved and crates hauled out of the way. The keepers had already transported the animals who were still alive and could walk. It took a crane to lift the larger animals who were too weak to walk on their own.

Several veterinarians and assistants worked quickly over each animal as it was placed in protective confinement. Some had to be tranquilized, but others were so emaciated they couldn't move. We couldn't see how many were dead inside the containers, but we knew it had been devastating. Elephants, lions, monkeys, parrots—all quiet with fear, hunger ,and despair. The shouting of the natives as they hurried around calling for someone to help with one animal or another, the fearful cries of the animals who still had strength to call out to each other. It was all too much to absorb.

I was glad I had not eaten breakfast for it would not have stayed down with the rising and overpowering stench of death.

Newer containers had been brought for the surviving animals where they could be tended to with caution and care. Fresh water had been hauled in but, some of the animals were too frail to drink. Some of the smaller animals had IV bags hanging from hooks to rehydrate them. Only hope and prayers could help the largest ones.

I was too overwhelmed to cry. I went to see what I could do to help the veterinarians.

The look of desperation on the faces of those large cats made me catch my breath. But it was the elephant's sad, droopy eyes that told me they didn't understand why anyone would do this to them. They walked with their heads hung low, and their trunks were feeling the ground in front of them. They had resigned themselves to the abuse and had no fight left in them.

Then I heard the soft whimpering cries that sounded like children—an almost silent weeping—but it was evident that there were more than one.

That is the container where I found Mr. Cleome. The horrors of how the animals were abused and abandoned did not compare to the horrors of this container, filled with young, half-naked boys shoved in the wooden slat box. It was not much different from the one Jake and I had been held captive, but compared to these conditions, ours had been the Ritz.

Almost a week with no food and little water. No chemical toilet behind a curtain, no beds. Emaciated figures were huddled next to each another in fear along the far wall. Eyes wide but too weak to cry.

Slave traders. I wanted to kill them all! Jake came to see what was in this last crate. When he saw and smelled the putrid order, he vomited and heaved and cried.

All I could do was hold him and let him cry. I wanted to cry, too, but I was too horrified to let go of my tears.

The children's crate had been in the back and was the last one opened. We were there to see them first. Someone had heard their cries, but they couldn't get to them until the animal crates were emptied and hauled out of the way. There were ten young boys in that crate. The look in their eyes will haunt me for the rest of my life. It was then I cried.

"Please forgive me for not warning you about the children," Mr. Cleome said as he walked over to us.

"I could not speak of it myself. The children I've rescued in the past were not in as horrifying a condition as this. Even though I know it happens, I had never seen it firsthand. If the potential "buyers" are suspicious about the patrol—or afraid customs will discover them—they leave the kids to die. The kids and the animals are just a commodity to these despicable people. They don't care what happens to them."

"This could've happened to us, couldn't it?" Jake asked.

Mr. Cleome did not answer right away. He was obviously struggling for composure.

Finally, he said, "Yes, you could have been left to die if they suspected I was not one of their typical buyers."

"What will happen to these kids?" I asked.

"They will be taken to hospitals in Bukabu to be examined. I have arranged for their keep and will pay for their medical needs. The local authorities will decide what to do with them."

"We were lucky. Very lucky. I see that now." Jake said.

"Try not to dwell on the past. What we do now, is more important. We have set up a temporary veterinary clinic here near the dock, to administer to the animals who are not strong enough to travel. The local veterinary clinics are not set up to deal with large or wild animals, so I radioed for some help. There are several Reserves and Nature parks in Tanzania who are sending some of their personnel to help and are willing to take a few of the animals. The other animals will be taken to my reserve when they are strong enough to travel."

"Your reserve?" Jake asked. "You mean to tell us the reserve you took us to is yours?"

"*Oui,* I thought I told you that."

Something in Jake had changed. Maybe it was necessary for us to experience this vile, horrendous act of inhumane abuse to understand more about our own experiences. When Jake flew us home, he no longer seemed afraid of flying. He paid more attention to the flight check, was more alert to his surroundings, and really seemed less annoyed with his world.

After what I had recently experienced, I was deeply grateful for the life I had been given. It is impossible to know why those poor children were captured and starved almost to their death. I would like to rationalize it, if for no other reason than to find some sense of peace. Hating the men who do these terrible things does no one any good. But looking for something good to come out of it helps with the healing. Eshe told me, "Hate only echoes hate within you. The person or thing you hate doesn't know—or care—how you feel, but the hate in you grows to no one's benefit and can only harm you. Hate is your personal disease."

Chapter 14

Time has a way of slipping by when you're busy. The old cliché that says "time flies when you're having fun" didn't seem to make as much sense as the words my mother used to say, "Time flies, so you might as well have fun."

"Where did the time go?" I said. "I can't believe I'm eighteen-years-old today!" My birthday celebration was extra special. Being of legal age, I was finally able to sample some of the wine our vineyards produced. Mr. Cleome suggested we just have a party without telling everyone it was my birthday so they wouldn't feel obligated to bring me presents. This suited me just fine. I had everything I needed or wanted and didn't want anyone to worry about whether their gift was suitable.

We hired a local professional band to play the latest tunes we listened to on the radio. I had made a few friends from town. So had Jake, but most of the people who attended the party lived or worked on the farm. It was difficult to make friends with people who lived in the city when I was more interested in the country lifestyle. Since I didn't attend the local schools, my close friends were Eshe, my tutors, and a few of the ranchers' kids. But the food was incredible, the wine flowed, and we all danced and had a wonderful time.

The following morning we got up a little later than usual since the party lasted until well past midnight.

At breakfast, Mr. Cleome said, "There are some decisions for you to make, *Mademoiselle* Kelly. Both of you actually," he added looking from me to Jake.

The hard physical work on the farm and the privileged lifestyle chiseled Jake into a strong, tanned, handsome young man. His sandy-brown hair was streaked blond from the sun, and his hazel green eyes looked more green than brown. He had grown to 5 foot 11 inches, taller than he expected, and he was the epitome of good health. I stayed petite but had the same hazel-green eyes that our mother passed on to us. My hair was also streaked with blonde in contrast to the tan of my face.

"You have both excelled in school, for which I am pleased. You have also been very loyal to me and worked hard on the farm. Two better children I could not have hoped for." Mr. Cleome fell silent for a moment, and then continued, "If my son had survived his illness, I might not have been given the opportunity to adopt you." He paused as he said the word *adopt* to emphasize the word.

140

"Sometimes life presents us with a different path than we thought we would take, and we don't always have choices about what changes we are forced to make. I would never have chosen to lose my wife or my son, but it happened anyway." Sadness clouded his eyes.

"You have experienced this as well when you lost your parents. We would never have chosen these losses, but because of them we have been given a new life—together." He paused to give us a chance to understand his words.

"There are a few things that I must tell you now. I find this to be more difficult than I thought it would be. Please allow me the opportunity to tell you everything before you interrupt. Agreed?" Mr. Cleome looked at both of us and waited for us to respond.

"This seems really serious," I said. "You have my full attention, but I am a little worried about what you could possibly tell us that is so difficult for you to say."

"Yes, *mes chéris*, what I am about to tell you may change how you feel about me and will certainly affect the rest of your lives."

Jake's eyes were wide and focused on Mr. Cleome. "You have my attention, too."

"Let me start by first telling you, I was so depressed over the loss of my family, I was about to let all my businesses go to ruin. I pretended to care, but there was no longer a reason to build my legacy with my son gone. I loved my wife more than the beating of my own heart. She lit up my day and gave me reason to breathe.

"When she told me we were to have a child, I didn't think I could be happier than I was at that exact moment. That was the happiest day of my life. Eight months later, we had to rush her to the hospital because the baby was coming early, and we could see there was a problem. She was in so much pain, we knew something was wrong. We feared for the baby. There were complications. I don't need to go into that right now, but my son took his first breath when my wife took her last."

Mr. Cleome fell silent remembering the pain of that day, so long ago.

"I lost my wife and my reason to live, but at the same moment, this baby boy, my son, gave me a reason to survive. Someone had to be there for him, something good had to come out of all that heartbreaking loss. I didn't know if I could bear to live without my wonderful, loving wife, but this delicate, innocent baby was here, and he needed someone. He needed me. I had to do what I could for him. It was not his fault my life would forever be changed.

"I kept myself busy and didn't accept any social

engagements in spite of the good intentions of my friends and associates to introduce me to potentially good female companions. I didn't want to marry again. No one could replace my beautiful wife or fill the void in my heart. I think now that I should have tried to love again, but I stayed so busy I didn't have the opportunity to meet anyone much less have the time to fall in love. I took my son everywhere to keep him close to me. I thought as long as he was with me he was safe. For several years I found great happiness with my son—until he got sick while we were on a long trip into the jungle, doing research. We were too far from civilization and proper medical attention to save him." Mr. Cleome stopped for a minute to clear his throat and gather his composure.

"The village we were in had a shaman who tried to heal him, but his medicine could not fight the disease that was starting to run rampant among his people. That shaman showed up at my door all these many miles away—nine years later. You may remember him; his name is Simba."

I gasped! "Simba?" I bolted up off the chair. I traveled back in my memory to the day we were rescued in the jungle after the plane crash. I remembered the native who brought me back to life with the bitter tea.

"He carried me out of the jungle on a sling and

nursed me back to health," I said. "How could he be a shaman? He was a guide for those terrible men who captured us and sold us...to you."

Jake was silent. I could tell he was trying to remember back to that horrible experience. Time does have a way of erasing bad memories.

"Wait, I don't understand. How did he get here when he was with us in the jungle?" I stood up and paced the floor trying to make sense of this story. "Why did he come to you?"

Mr. Cleome gave us both time to absorb this news, but knowing he could not explain it satisfactorily, he said, "Most people think a shaman is only a silly man with a scary mask, rattles, feathers, and face paint. But other people believe in their ability to heal, change shape—and travel great distances with the blink of an eye."

"Now, wait a minute," Jake had to interrupt. "You are telling us Simba came to you at the same time he was with us? And he can change shapes? What did he become, a bird?"

I stopped pacing so suddenly everyone looked over to where I stood. Shivers ran up my spine, and I could feel the hair on the back of my neck stand up. Goosebumps raised on my arms so large Jake could see them from the chair he was sitting in.

"Sis, what is wrong?"

"Or a leopard?" I said.

"What do you mean? What are you saying, Sis," Jake said.

"Oh, Jake, do you remember me telling you about my dreams when the black leopard came to me? He first came when I was sick in the jungle, just before those men rescued us. Remember?" I added, "Oh, I might not have told you that. But remember just before we were put on that ship I told you about the leopard who gave me a ride on his back? He was warning us about what would happen."

"Well, yeah, I remember that silly dream, but what are you suggesting? That the leopard was Simba? Ridiculous!" Jake stood up and walked over to me. "Have you lost your mind?"

I blew air out of my pursed lips and shrugged. "I don't know, Jake. I don't know." I looked at Mr. Cleome hoping for a better explanation.

"Sorry, I don't have a reasonable answer. You will have to sort through that yourself." Mr. Cleome continued, "There is more to tell you, and you might not like what I have to say. Please sit down, and let me finish."

Jake and I went back to our chairs and waited for Mr. Cleome to continue. I was struggling with the idea that Simba could have been the leopard that appeared in my dreams.

Sadness once again shadowed Mr. Cleome's face. He continued the story. "When I heard there were two orphaned white children about to be sold as slaves, I told Simba to tell those men I would buy you sight unseen, and I would pay a handsome price if you were not hurt in any way. I called my pilot and told him to get the plane ready; we would leave within the hour."

Neither of us spoke, and I could tell Jake was as confused as I.

"Now here is the part you are not going to like." He began with a little hesitation. "When Simba came to me that night, he handed me your passports to show me who you were."

"Our passports! Our passports?" Jake suddenly bolted up off his chair causing it to fall backward onto the floor. "You had our passports all the time? You knew we were Americans, but you still treated us like slaves? You let them put us in those cages? You lied to us!" He was about to run out of the room in a rage of disbelief. "You stole us!"

"Wait, son," Mr. Cleome shouted. It was the first time he called Jake *son*. Jake froze in his tracks. He looked hurt and confused. Tears formed in his eyes, and his shoulders shook with the grief he had buried for so long.

"Please, sit down. There is more," Mr. Cleome

said quietly.

Jake was breathless as he staggered to pick up his chair. His expression changed from confusion to sorrow. "What more could you tell us that would be any worse than what you have already said?" he said with bitterness. He sat on the edge of his chair and looked like he was ready to run out of the room.

I was in shock and couldn't speak. Is it possible Simba was a shapeshifter? A shaman and a leopard? He was the one who stole our passports? It was just so unbelievable I couldn't think straight. The memories flooded back to our time in the shipping crate and how disgusting that was. I also thought of those other children who had not been treated even that well. I just sat there in disbelief, my mind was filled with many pictures, visions, and memories. I shook my head to hear what Mr. Cleome was saying next.

"Remember I told you I had to pretend to be a slave driver? If I had not treated you the way I did, it is likely you would have been taken to the auction block with the intention of getting more money from someone else."

Mr. Cleome continued, "An attempt on my life was likely, and it is also possible someone would have attempted to kill you out of rage. I doubt that would have happened because you were worth more money alive than dead, but there are some people who work in this market who would not have cared.

"It is not easy to understand the way of greedy men." Mr. Cleome said. "One of my foundations helps to support several wilderness areas where it is illegal to hunt or capture wild animals. I cannot stop the sale of these animals, but I can provide a place for some of them to be safe. You have seen that I have prepared a home for many children, but you are the first I have chosen to live with me as family."

"There is so much about you and your work we don't know," I said.

"In time, my child, hopefully, you will want to know more, but for now, I must tell you something else." Mr. Cleome continued, "Once I had you safely at home with me, I took a trip. You may remember I left for a few days right after you came here."

"Yes, Eshe told us you had a lot of work to catch up on," I said.

"That is true, but I had to do one thing first. I had to find your relatives if there were any."

"You what?" Jake stood up again hardly able to contain his anger.

"Please Jake, I asked you to bear with me and let me tell you everything," Mr. Cleome pleaded. "You can then decide what you want to do with the information once it is yours."

Jake took a deep breath and let it out in a rush of

fury. "I'm sorry. I...I..."

"I know this is not easy to understand, but please allow to me explain. Your passports gave your parents' address, and there was an emergency number to contact if anything happened to them. That number was for your Aunt Emma. I flew to the States to meet her and to tell her in person what had happened. I didn't think this was something that should be done over the phone or in a telegram."

"You talked to Aunt Emma? And she allowed you to keep us?" I interrupted. "I can't believe this! Didn't she want us?" I fought against tears that welled up inside me. I felt so betrayed.

"I know all of this is difficult for you to hear, but again, please let me finish," Mr. Cleome pleaded. "I called ahead and told her who I was and that I had news from her sister. I didn't tell her what had happened until I met her face to face. When I told her about the accident, she fell in a heap, crying so hard she could hardly catch her breath. Her lungs were so bad from smoking cigarettes that she just coughed and sputtered. Your Uncle Will was no better off. I told them both that you two kids were rescued and safe. I didn't tell them about the slavery problem. I didn't think they needed to know that at the time, but I did make a deal with them."

"A deal? You made a deal with our only relatives? What kind of deal? Did they sell us out?" Jake couldn't help asking.

"No, Jake, they did not sell you out. What I proposed to them is that I would raise you as my own children and give you every advantage that my love and money could provide. I told them about my son, and that I had no one to leave my fortune. I wanted to adopt you both, and if they would agree to allow this to happen, I would, in turn, send them photographs and a report on how you were doing every few months. At first, they did not agree to allow me to keep you. They wanted you to come home and live with them."

Mr. Cleome stood up and walked across the room for some lemonade. He brought a glass for himself and one for each of us. He took a sip and continued.

"I hated to be rude to them, but I pointed out that their house was not a healthy place to raise kids with the second-hand smoke and the brown sticky tobacco residue on everything. I thought it was essential for you both to stay with me. I was being a little selfish, but I had your best interests at heart. You came to me for a reason. I know this to be true, and I was going to do my best to allow the plan to unfold."

Mr. Cleome frowned but continued, "I told them they would probably not live long enough to see you children grow up at the rate they were killing themselves. I told them if you were both raised in their house, you, too, would get sick from their smoke. It was the ugly truth, and I apologized for being so blunt."

Neither Jake nor I could speak. I remembered our aunt and uncle smoked a lot, but the thought never occurred to me that it was killing them or how it could be dangerous for our health.

"Jake and I once talked about living with them if we ever got rescued and went home. I remember not liking to be in their house for long," I finally said. "It really smelled bad in there."

"Yeah, I remember the stinky ashtrays full of cigarette butts," Jake nodded.

"But they said it was okay for you to keep us forever?" I asked with tears forming in my eyes.

"I told them that I would give you all the love and benefits I could provide. I would keep them informed about you both, and when you were old enough to make your own decisions, I would tell you the truth about what happened. If you wanted to go back to the United States, I would pay for your trip."

Mr. Cleome looked at me and said, "Today, my dear, is your eighteenth birthday. You are old enough to make your own decisions now. Your birthday present from me is a trip back to Orlando, Florida, if you want to go. You both may go, of course."

I couldn't speak. My throat felt like it would burst open if I tried to talk. Even taking a breath was difficult. My chest felt like a ton of bricks was sitting on me, waiting for me to exhale and crush any life left in me. My head swam with an assortment of emotions from happiness to know our aunt and uncle were still alive to anger from being tossed aside by them and to relief that we were given such a beautiful home by the man who gave us a gift of life with love, respect, and opportunity.

"There is one more thing I must tell you," Mr. Cleome added. "I filed the papers to adopt you both if you are willing. I thought you might want to keep your last names, out of respect to your parents."

"You want to adopt us?" Jake asked. "But why? We were working to pay you back for buying us."

"No, you were working to develop a proper education and a foundation to understand what you would inherit from me when I die. I want you to know I have done everything for you because I love you both. I have waited so long to say those words aloud. I love you," he repeated as his eyes reddened, and his lips quivered.

Tears rolled out of my eyes, no longer willing to remain bottled up. I ran over to the man sitting there. He was also crying. I threw my arms about him and cried so hard my body shook. "I, I, I love you, too,

Mr... ah, Mr..." it didn't seem right to call this man by his surname when he was offering to be my father.

"*Pardon moi, ma chère.* My name is Édouard Cleome the Third. Yes, there is a little royalty in my background, but that doesn't mean much here in South Africa. I would love it if someday you could call me *le père*. That is French for father. But I will settle for Edward if you are more comfortable with a name."

"*Le père,*" I liked how it sounded and said, "*Oui, Le père,* I like that!"

"If you don't mind, sir, I would be more comfortable calling you Edward for now," Jake said. He stood up and shook hands with his benefactor and newly acclaimed father.

"*Bon!*" he said, "I will honor your wishes. Now, we have plans to make." Edward Cleome stood up. "I need to attend to a little personal business. While I do, I would like for you both to take a little time to digest all you have learned today. You have no idea how wonderful it feels to have the burden of this truth out in the open now. We will talk more tomorrow, but for tonight I want you to think about what you want to do now that you know you have options."

Chapter 15

I didn't think I would ever get to sleep with all that happened today. *How will I know what to do?* I asked myself. When sleep finally came, it was a deep sleep that carried me off to my dreams.

"You asked for me?" the deep voice growled.

I turned around, and staring at me was the black leopard, his tail swaying, waiting for a reply.

"Oh, did I? I don't remember asking for you, but I am happy to see you again. You have been watching out for me, haven't you?"

"I am always with you and have been for longer than you know."

"May I ask you a few questions?"

"You may," the leopard replied.

"How did you know Mr. Cleome? Why did you go to him to rescue us?"

"He has already told you about the day his son fell sick. I was in that village and knew his heart would be broken. He has done so much for the village people all over our country, he is a man of great value to our people and animals. When I knew you

were coming, I waited."

"What do you mean you knew we were coming?" I asked. "That was a long time before we even knew we would come to Africa."

"You must know by now that more happens in our lives than can easily be explained," the leopard answered. "If you trust in your spirit, you will know that for everything there is a reason."

"But what could possibly be the reason for my parents to die?"

"The reason is not the question, the answer is in the outcome."

"But why did they have to die?" I cried.

"When you know about Spirit, you will understand there is no death."

"Let me ask you one more question. What should I do, now?"

"Listen to your Spirit," the leopard said as he turned to leave.

"Wait, wait. Don't leave me now. I don't understand what it is I should do?"

The leopard turned and said, "It is time now."

"Time? What do you mean it is time now? Time for what?" I begged.

"It is time to open all your presents." And he was gone.

I woke up with a start and took a breath of air so deep I felt like this was the first full breath I had taken in a long time.

It was not quite daylight, but by the sounds of the birds, I knew morning was close. My dream was puzzling—what did it mean? Why did the leopard say it was time to open all my presents? With the sudden realization, I glanced over to my dresser where I kept the few things that were left from my life with my parents. "The present from Mom!" I gasped. "It must be time to open that present from Mom."

For the first time, I held the precious package in my hands without crying. I was no longer sad as I held the small box and looked at the fancy silky material. I was actually excited to see what my mother had bought for me so long ago.

Just then Jake knocked at my bedroom door. "Sis, are you okay?"

"Yes, Jake, come in. I'm glad you're here."

Jake turned on the overhead light and saw me holding the mysterious present I had kept for so long.

"What is going on?" he asked. "I heard voices."

"I had another dream about the leopard," I said not looking up from the precious gift in my hand. "He told me it was time to open my present."

Jake watched me untie the tattered satin bow.

"It seems so obsolete after all these years. I was only twelve then or almost twelve. I can't imagine what Mom would have given me then that would matter now, but I know I have to let go of her. And I can only let go when I open the gift."

The silk scarf fell away, and a tiny velvet box waited to be opened. I took a deep breath and opened the rain-stained box.

"Oh!" I exclaimed. "Oh, my!"

"What is it, Sis? What's in the box?"

"Look, Jake," I said. Tears stung my eyes. "Look! It's a necklace with a gold, heart-shaped locket. Look inside—there are tiny little pictures of Mom and Dad!" I cried as I handed the locket to my brother.

"I was starting to forget what they looked like," Jake said as his eyes, too, began to tear up. "There's something inscribed on the back."

"What does it say?" I asked.

"It says, 'We give you the gift of opportunity.'"

Chapter 16

I gently rubbed the locket that hung on a gold chain around my neck, as I waited for the airplane to land in Orlando, Florida. Edward Cleome had given us two one-way tickets each. We could use the return flight if or when we wanted, or we could tear them up. The decision was ours. But first I needed to see my only living relatives. Would they recognize me? Will I know them? Will they be happy to see us both? The excitement of being back in Florida was almost too much to hold inside. I couldn't wait to get off the airplane. I wanted to run down the corridor and grab my aunt and uncle and hold them so tight they couldn't let go. It was a relief to be here after so many years away and not knowing if I would ever set foot on US soil again. My throat was dry, but my palms were sweaty. I wanted to clutch Jake's hand and hold it tight. But I couldn't let go of the armrest.

Finally, the plane landed and taxied to the gate. It was strange to hear people talking in English as they grabbed their bags from the overhead bin. Most of the flight attendants were white and spoke without an accent. It felt strange to blend in with the crowd instead of standing out with our pale skin. Here we were nobody—instead of the rich plantation man's kids. No one in Africa treated us differently on purpose, but there was always some reserve in their attitudes—reserve from everyone except Eshe, and, of course, Edward. There, we were strangers in a strange land. But here, we were strangers in a familiar land.

While we waited for the exit door to open, Jake said, "You go on ahead, Sis, I'll get our carry-ons from overhead. I know how excited you are."

"Thanks, Jake! I can hardly wait. Thanks for getting my bag."

I walked as fast as I could to the baggage claim area.

"Aunt Emma! Uncle Will!" I hollered. "You look great."

"Why, my dear, I would know you anywhere! Mr. Cleome sent us photographs of you both all the time. We saw you doing all kinds of fun things on the farm and in that mansion! Oh, y'all must have felt like a pea in a bucket rattling around that huge place."

"We got used to it. You get to know a place pretty well when you have to dust and polish furniture," I said, laughing.

"You had to do all that work? Why I would've thought...."

"No, Edward expected us to work so we could appreciate what we had," I explained.

"Where's Jake? Didn't he come with you?" Uncle Will asked.

"Oh, he'll be here. He offered to bring my carry-on luggage. He knew I couldn't wait to see you. Oh, there he is!" I shouted, "Jake over here!"

Jake came to us with a smile, his hand stretched out to shake. "Uncle Will, how nice to see you," Jake greeted. "Aunt Emma you look radiant!" He kissed her on the cheek.

"Is this that same snot nose kid we used to know?" Uncle Will joked. "Come here boy, and give your ol' uncle a bear hug." I could see Jake was a little uncomfortable with the long embrace from a man he barely knew. We hadn't hugged many people in the last six years. It wasn't until recently we accepted Edward Cleome as family, so I knew this display of affection was strange for Jake. I welcomed it, but it was strange just the same.

"Let's get your luggage and head home. I have a traditional Southern-style dinner just waiting for you." Emma beamed. "Y'all still like good ol' southern greens, black-eyed peas, and cornbread don't ya?"

"It's seems like a lifetime since I've eaten good Southern cooking. You bet we still like it," Jake said as he hugged his aunt.

Will brought the car around, loaded our luggage, and drove away from the airport.

"Orlando has changed quite a bit since we were here last," I said. "I can't believe how much it has grown. Do you still live in the same place?"

"No, didn't you know?" Uncle Will said.

"Know what?" Jake asked from the back seat.

"Well, Mr. Cleome came to see us, just after...well, you know," Aunt Emma started.

"We know. He told us about coming to see you, but what does that have to do with you moving?"

"Well, dear," Aunt Emma explained. "He told us it would not be healthy for y'all to live with us, with the smoke an' all, so we took some of that money he sent and went to a health spa to get cleaned up from the addiction to those dang cigarettes."

"What money?" I asked.

"Oh, didn't he tell you? With the photos, he also sent a check—just about every three months, wasn't it Will?"

"Why did he send you money—payment for us?" Jake sneered.

"Oh, no my darling, you have it all wrong," Aunt Emma was quick to say. "He didn't offer to buy you from us. We could see that what he offered you would be so much more than we could possibly have given you. He just sent us half of your wages. He said you were paying off a debt. We didn't know what that meant, but we decided if you were giving us a gift, we would use it to get healthy. We live near the beach now. The air is so much better than in the city. Your Uncle Will has started a nursery and grows all sorts of native plants for folks who do landscaping. Remember how much your mother loved plants?" Emma added.

"Well, I'll be...." Jake said. "He sent you half of what would have been our wages if we had known we were getting paid. We just thought we were paying him back for buying us from the slave traders."

"Slave traders?" Uncle Will exclaimed. "What kind of nonsense are you talking about, boy?"

"Oh, never mind," I interrupted. "That was something else." I certainly did not want to talk about that terrible time so long ago with my aunt and uncle. They didn't need those images in their minds.

"I wonder what he did with the other half of our so-called wages," Jake wondered out loud.

"Well, he said something about your half going into a trust fund or something to help you get started in your lives if y'all came back to Florida to live," Emma explained. "He said you might not want to stay in South Africa with him after you heard about what he did with your passports and stuff."

Jake gave me a sideways glance, but his face didn't reveal anything to me about how he was reacting to this news.

"Here we are—home sweet home," Aunt Emma said as we pulled into the driveway. Their yard was like a jungle with all the palms, ferns, bushes, and trees.

"This is beautiful!" I exclaimed. "Mom would have loved seeing you two do this! I worried about you both so much."

"Well, her spirit is always with us," Emma said with a smile. "I used to listen to her all the time, telling me what to grow," she laughed. "Let's go in. I just need to put the cornbread in the oven and heat up the greens and beans. Y'all still like pork chops, don't you?"

After dinner, we sat around until late at night talking about all that had happened to each other— or almost all. There were some things I didn't think we needed to tell.

When the morning songbirds sang their excitement for the new day, I just lay there listening to their cheery sounds. The realization of being back in Florida after all those years away was a little overpowering. I wanted that moment to last as long as possible.

"Home. I'm finally home," I whispered. "Well,

sort of." I barely knew these people who were my closest kin. Everything has changed so much.

The smell of freshly brewed coffee gave me the incentive to get out of bed and greet the day. "Morning, Auntie," I said when I went into the kitchen.

"About time you got up, sleepy head," she chuckled. "Uncle Will had a delivery to make and said he would eat breakfast when he got back, figuring you'd need to sleep in after the long flight. Jake was already up and wanted to go with him. Will welcomed the help, of course. He was happy to spend some time with the boy. This'll give us a chance to talk, too, my dear. Coffee?"

"I'd love some, thanks."

"How does it feel to be home?" Emma asked.

"Well, I am not quite sure yet, Aunt Emma, I feel disoriented. Maybe it's jet lag, but I feel divided. I'm happy to see you, but it feels so strange to be here, and yet it also feels familiar. Like *déjà vu*."

"I gotta ask you a question, Kelly. It's bothered your Uncle Will and me for a long time. I hope you don't mind me being so direct. Do you hate us for letting Mr. Cleome raise you?"

I could see this was a deep concern for my Aunt, whose eyes welled up with tears to match the ones in my own eyes. "No Auntie, I don't hate you, far from it. I wondered all those years about you and how you must have worried about what happened to us when Mom didn't write or call. You must have thought we were all dead."

"I see there is much Mr. Cleome didn't tell you," Emma said.

"What do you mean?"

"We assumed you knew he had visited us after the crash." Emma began to cry. "Since we never got a letter from y'all, we thought you were mad at us for letting you stay there. We were so afraid we would never see you again. Mr. Cleome said he would give you the choice, but so many years went by, we thought you didn't care about us and decided to stay there."

"Oh, Aunt Emma! No! We didn't know he had visited you until just a few weeks ago." I was so choked up I could hardly speak. "If we had known he'd been here—we would have insisted he let us go. We would've figured out a way to come home if it was the last thing we did. We didn't know about any of this until my birthday when he told us.

"I tried to mail a letter to you, but I didn't know your exact address. I stole a piece of paper, envelope, and stamp from the office one day while I was dusting. I addressed it to both of you in Orlando, Florida. The letter was never returned, so I didn't know if you got it or not. I figured if you cared about us, you would have written back."

"No dear, we never got that letter from you. When Mr. Cleome wrote to us and sent the photos and checks, he never gave a return address. The checks were money orders that we couldn't trace. As much as we wanted to write to you, we couldn't, but he was true to his word about keeping us informed on your lives. So we had to accept his reasons. We didn't have much choice."

I realized if I had known how to reach my aunt I wouldn't have adapted so well to my situation, especially in the beginning when I was so lonesome.

"Jake would certainly not have tolerated staying there. He so badly wanted to come home. I understand now why he didn't tell us about everything. Thanks for telling me now."

"I gotta ask one more question, dear," Emma said with a little hesitation.

"Go ahead and ask. I would prefer to be totally honest and open."

"What do you plan to do now? Will you stay here in Florida?"

The door burst open, and Will and Jake entered the room. "Emma, do you have them grits made yet? We menfolk are sure hungry," Will said, laughing.

"I had almost forgotten about grits." Jake laughed, too. "That would sure taste good!"

Chapter 17

Listen to your Spirit. This was the only answer that came to me that night when I asked myself, "What will I do now?"

"I don't know what that means!" I silently pleaded. "How do I decide what to do?"

Morning came with no more visits from my leopard spirit. I felt like I had been abandoned again.

"I need help!" I said looking up at the ceiling.

"What, dear?" Emma said as she passed by my room. "Were you talking to me?"

"Morning, Auntie. No, I was talking to myself. I'll be out in a minute."

I showered and dressed in shorts and a sleeveless blouse.

"What would you like to do today, kids?" Emma asked during breakfast.

"I would love to go to the beach if you're not too busy," I said. "It's been so long since I've walked on Florida sand."

"Kelly, you have to realize your uncle Will and I might be dead by now if it weren't for you and Jake. Anything in this whole world you want, you just let us know. We owe y'all more than you can ever know."

"I don't understand," Jake said.

"If it hadn't been for the wake-up call from Mr. Cleome about our smokin' and for gettin' those checks from your wages, we wouldn't have quit those dang cigarettes and found a new life for ourselves. The damage has been done to our lungs already, I'm afraid, but we can at least believe we've added years to what life we have left. We owe our lives to you kids."

"Yeah, and if you want to go to the beach, that is what we will do," Will added. "I have been preparin' my customers for weeks. As soon as we heard you were coming, I told them, 'order what you need, now, as I'll be too busy when they get here.' Yesterday morning was the last delivery I had already promised."

I watched as Aunt Emma packed a basket with food. "A picnic lunch is a perfect idea, Aunt Emma. I always get hungry at the beach."

"Must be that salty air and the smell of rotten fish," Uncle Will joked.

After a swim and some body surfing, I stretched out on my beach towel to sun dry. Jake flirted with some bikini-clad girls who seemed to think he was the most handsome man on the beach. Maybe he was.

Will brought his fishing pole and was busy casting his line when Emma brought out sandwiches, fried chicken, potato salad, chips, and a bowl of fresh cut fruit.

I rolled over on my side in time to see something fuzzy dart behind a clump of sea oats.

"Look, Aunt Emma, a kitten!" It was obviously scared and hungry. The hope of getting a piece of crust or something to eat from these beach visitors brought it out of hiding.

"It's hungry. Do we have something to give it?" I asked.

"Let's see here—I made tuna sandwiches, it must have smelled it a long ways off. Here's a sandwich. I made plenty."

I took a bite from the sandwich as I slowly sat up. I pinched off a piece of bread with lots of tuna and offered it to the kitten. Hungry, yes; brave, no. It ventured out of hiding, but it scurried back when I moved. I tossed a little piece of tuna close to the weeds and watched as the kitten slowly crept out from his cover, looking around for any of the other beach cats that could steal his snack. He grabbed it in his teeth and darted away again.

Patiently I offered another piece of my sandwich, and the kitten came a little closer for another snack. I sat there for half an hour cooing to the kitten and tossing tidbits of food.

"I know what it feels like to be hungry and scared," I said to the kitten.

Hunger finally conquered fear, and the kitten came close enough this time to eat the food in front of me. Slowly stretching my hand, I was able to touch it, briefly, before the kitten's fear welled up and it fled. "Aw, it's so skinny, Auntie. It must be starving."

"Yeah, there are lots of abandoned and gone-wild cats out here," Emma said. "People don't get their cats spayed or neutered, so they keep breeding and making more hungry kittens. It's a pity someone doesn't do something for these poor wild animals instead of letting them starve to death."

"What did you say?" I gasped.

"It's a pity they let these little, wild animals starve to death," Emma replied. "Why?"

The memory of those wild animals left in cages to die of hunger or thirst caused my eyes to burn.

"Kitty, Kitty," I said to choke back my tears. "Here Kitty, here's another bite of food."

The kitten came out again and ate the offering. "Oh, my goodness; look at you," I said. "If you aren't the prettiest little kitty I've ever seen—and those big yellow eyes—they remind me of someone."

Tears flowed from my eyes as I stared at this little black kitten, remembering another feline that came to visit me a long time ago. I stroked his shiny black fur as I gave him more tuna. This time the kitten didn't scurry away, it looked up at me with a soft "Mew?"

"Aunt Emma, what do you think about cats?"

"Oh, I like them fine, but we've never thought about having a pet. Why?"

"Well, if this little kitty will let me, I'd like to bring it home with us. I've already given it a name: Simba. May I give it a little of that fried chicken?"

The smell of chicken made the kitten brave enough to allow me to get closer. It devoured the meat so fast it growled with greed. I had to be careful to keep my fingers away from those little gnashing sharp teeth as the kitten ate everything I offered. Finally, I was able to grab him by the nape of his neck fur.

"Well, little Simba, I'm afraid I'll have to hold you captive in Aunt Emma's picnic basket until we get you to your new home," I cooed. "It's for your own good, I promise. I'll give you the gift of opportunity for a good life too. And thanks, Simba, for the answer to my question about what I should do."

Chapter 18

At dinner that night, I announced. "I've made a decision. I would like to stay here a few more weeks, but I want to go back to South Africa. I know what I want to do. Saving that little kitten at the beach made me realize how important it is to save as many trapped and abused wild animals as I can. I know Mr. Cleome...ahhh...Edward has supported several game preserves, and I would like to work at one of them and rescue wild animals from the illegal traders. I think we can also hold the traders who have permits to trap them accountable to provide a more humane environment."

"You want to go back?" Jake asked.

"I do. I didn't know it until this afternoon. I really love Edward. He feels like a father to me, and I know everything he did for us was because he loved us. I feel like this is something I'm supposed to do...something in my destiny. For some reason, I was taken to Africa. I can't explain it. I feel drawn to the animals."

"Well, dear, if that is what you want to do, then you must," Aunt Emma replied. "Maybe your Uncle Will and I can come visit you sometime. I'd love to see where y'all have been living."

"You go, honey, someone has to stay here and tend to our own little jungle," Will said with a wink. "I never took to flying much; don't want to get stuck in that flying bullet of a machine. I had enough flying in the war, don't care to do it again."

"What do you think, Jake?" I asked. "Have you made any decision yet?"

"Well, Sis. I'd like to stay here a while and think about what I want. I have an idea, and if I go for it, I need this break now, because I'll be too busy later on to play."

"You can always work for us here at the nursery," Will suggested. "You know you will inherit all of this someday," Will said as his laughter turned into a coughing spasm.

"Thanks, Unc. I would be happy to work here for a while to pay for my room and vittles." He smiled and winked at Aunt Emma. Jake knew he had his own money now, but he wanted to work for his board. "Besides I met a girl on the beach that I would like to see again. Who knows? Maybe she is 'the one,'" he said, only half-joking.

"I have an idea, Kelly," Jake said. "Why don't you give my ticket to Aunt Emma so she can fly back with you? I'll buy my own return ticket when I'm ready."

"Oh, my, I was half kidding about going to South

Africa!" Aunt Emma exclaimed. "Who'd take care of your uncle if I left?"

"Oh, don't worry none about me, woman. Jake and I can be bachelors for a while and take care of ourselves—of course, we will miss your fine cooking, but we can get along. You deserve a break—go on to Africa. It'll be good for ya!"

"Oh, mercy me! I guess he wants to get rid of me." Emma smiled, "I've never been out of Florida, and now I'm going to the other side of the world! Guess I'd better buy a suitcase!"

At the airport, Jake gave me a big hug. It felt strange to say goodbye to him—we had depended on each other for so many years. I fought against the tears that threatened to fall. "Keep in touch, Bro! I'll sure miss you. It's hard to imagine not seeing your funny face around."

"Well, don't get too used to it, Sis. You never know when I might show up. I'm thinking pretty seriously about going to medical school and studying infectious diseases like Dad did. I don't know where I will study just yet, but I would like to feel my freedom for a while before I decide."

I gave my uncle a hug and fought back tears of sadness and joy. I knew I could return any time I wanted, but it was possible I would never see him again. My destiny was sealed when I listened to my Spirit and returned home—home to South Africa.

Before I entered the security gates, I called back to Jake, "Tell little Simba kitty I will see him in my dreams."

Epilogue

Edward was elated that I returned. He asked if I'd like to show the reserve to my aunt, which, of course, I was anxious to do. She was a little hesitant but finally agreed after we told her there were more dangerous critters in Florida with the poisonous snakes, rabid skunks, alligators, and black widow spiders.

When we toured the facilities this time, I saw it with new eyes—almost like a vision, crystal clear—and knew this is where I was supposed to be.

I decided to attend the University of Pretoria, one of the top teaching and research institutions in Africa. After I got my Doctorate of Veterinary Medicine, I went on to get my degrees in Zoology.

Father Edward fell ill after I graduated from Veterinary School. He'd been sick for a while but kept it from everyone except Eshe. She, being a medicine woman, treated Edward, but he told her to keep it between them. We all die at some time, and it was Edward's time. But before he left us, he showed me his will. There were provisions for Jake and me. He had left the reserve in trust to me with enough capital to keep it running for many years. With the help of a few generous donors and visitors, we manage to keep the animals safe and rescue many more each year from illegal trappers and poachers. Some we relocate and some we keep.

An extraordinary thing happened the night Edward died. I heard what sounded like a wild cat's roar. It was an eerie sound, mournful. It reflected exactly what I felt, but I couldn't tell from where the sound came. Not just once but several times, I heard the roar, which seems a little strange there in the city where there are no lions or—leopards. I got a call a few minutes later from the reserve saying the lions nearby were making a lot of noise. One of the keepers got on the phone and said, "Lady, the lions are crying."

I told him Mr. Cleome just died, and the keeper said, "The lions—they know."

This morning as I was feeding the animals, I saw a black leopard in the shadows, as I do from time to time. It was Simba checking in on me.